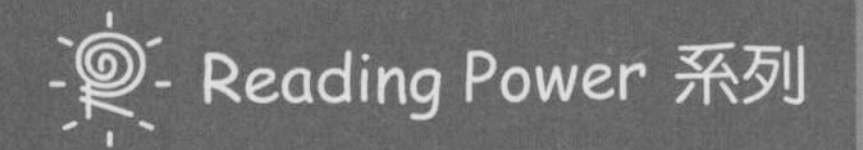

★ 108 課綱、全民英檢中級適用
★ 可搭配 108 課綱加深加廣選修課程及多元選修課程

英文閱讀 G.O., G.O., G.O.!

(二版)

附電子朗讀音檔、翻譯與解析

編著者
應惠蕙
學歷／國立臺灣師範大學英語學系研究所碩士
經歷／華東臺商子女學校教師
新竹女中退休教師

審訂者
Peter John Wilds
學歷／Degree in English literature from the University of Newcastle-upon-Tyne (UK)
經歷／ESL teacher in Taiwan for twenty-five years; freelancer

三民書局

序

知識，就是希望；閱讀，就是力量。

在這個資訊爆炸的時代，應該如何選擇真正有用的資訊來吸收？
在考場如戰場的競爭壓力之下，應該如何儲備實力，漂亮地面對挑戰？
身為地球村的一份子，應該如何增進英語實力，與世界接軌？

學習英文的目的，就是要讓自己在這個資訊爆炸的時代之中，突破語言的藩籬，站在吸收新知的制高點之上，以閱讀獲得力量，以知識創造希望！

針對在英文閱讀中可能面對的挑戰，我們費心規劃 Reading Power 系列叢書，希望在學習英語的路上助您一臂之力，讓您輕鬆閱讀、快樂學習。

誠摯希望在學習英語的路上，這套 Reading Power 系列叢書將伴隨您找到閱讀的力量，發揮知識的光芒！

給讀者的話

閱讀英文文章時，你是否經常有找不到全文或段落主旨的困難？寫英文作文時，你是否也常得到「全文毫無組織」的評語？如果你遇到以上問題，圖形組織圖 (graphic organizers) 就是來幫助你解決以上困難，成為你增進英文閱讀與寫作能力的利器。

I. 什麼是圖形組織圖？

圖形組織圖 (其中部分亦稱為腦圖、概念圖、思維導圖或心智圖等) 為一種將知識、概念或構思以視覺圖像呈現出來的圖像式思考輔助工具，幫助讀者將表面不相關的訊息轉化，並濃縮成一目了然的圖形。產出的視覺圖形將複雜的訊息以簡單易懂的方式呈現。不論線性或非線性的資料、訊息及構思，在轉化成圖形的過程中，都能增加讀者對主題的深入了解，因為繪出圖形的過程中，讀者必須專注於每個項目間的關係，並檢查其附加意義，也必須決定項目的優先順序，才能產出正確的圖形組織圖。

II. 圖形組織圖的優點：

(一) 可激發創造力、思考力，產出許多新觀點；

(二) 可提升讀者興趣及學習動機，並幫助記憶文章內容；

(三) 可將文章的組織與發展結構視覺化，進而釐清資料，幫助組織概念，加強理解；

(四) 可增進課堂教學過程中，學生合作學習、分享討論，並促進師生互動。

III. 圖形組織圖的功用：

圖形組織圖主要用於英文學習中的閱讀及寫作兩方面。事實上，就連聽力與口說也能利用圖形組織圖增加學習成效。除了一般英文自學，在英文教學歷程中，圖形組織圖的不同功能也能在教學上增添助益，以下為幾種教學上的建議：

(一) 作為教學前的導引、教學中的回顧及教學後的摘要與統整

教學前，可利用圖形組織圖，引導學生運用與主題相關的先備知識，將學習注意力集中在更深入的內容，或引導學生推論與預測後續將要學習的部分。也可以先呈現教學內容的圖形組織圖，讓學生可以預測文章內容。

教師也可在教學中，利用圖形組織圖引導學生回顧已學習的部分，增進對內容的理解與記憶。教學後，圖形組織圖可統整學習內容，協助學生了解內容摘要。教師可讓學生填入未完成的組織圖，也可師生共同討論、繪製組織圖，藉此讓學生獲得整體性的知識並作為複習與回憶的工具。

(二) 激發構思並促進腦力激盪

利用圖形組織圖將思維視覺化的特性，不論於閱讀的預測活動 (prediction) 或寫作前的腦力激盪 (brainstorming)，都能簡單地幫助學生看到自己的想法，也能輕易地由一個思考中心發展出許多節點，每個節點又可形成另一個思考中心，以此類推繼續發展下去。於閱讀預測活動時，學生可將自己的想法無限延伸，增加推測力及創造性的思考能力；而於寫作時，組織圖能激盪出更多想法，便於篩檢出最適合主題的文章細節。

(三) 提升學生閱讀理解力

圖形組織圖可協助教師訓練學生的閱讀能力。閱讀前，學生如果熟悉文章的架構，便較不易對內容理解錯誤，也可加快閱讀速度，因此教師可利用圖形組織圖同時訓練學生的閱讀理解力與閱讀速度。閱讀後，學生可先討論、分析，再填入圖形組織圖，經過訓練，學生甚至可自行繪出符合文章架構的組織圖，增進其分析思考的能力。

(四) 協助學習英文作文架構

英文作文架構與中文作文不同，不少學生受中文影響，無法寫出開門見山、脈絡清楚的文章。然而，不論記敘文、描寫文、程序文、比較文、說明文或議論文等，都有其相對應的圖形組織圖。教師可先讓學生熟悉不同種類的文章及其圖形組織圖，接下來根據要寫的主題讓學生填入相對應的組織圖，待學生能完全掌控各類組織圖後，可讓學生根據主題自行利用圖形組織圖腦力激盪，整理出文章架構及細節，再開始寫作。

(五) 練習聽力與口說的工具

練習段落聽力時，可讓學生先看聽力內容的圖形組織圖，以了解大意，之後再聽相關內容會更容易聽懂；也可於聽完後，讓學生填入組織圖，以確認學生聽懂大意。練習口說時，可利用講稿內容的圖形組織圖幫助記憶講稿，忘稿時也能根據架構回憶內容。

(六) 評鑑學生學習成果

不論圖形組織圖應用在聽、說、讀、寫哪一方面，都有一重要目的——評量。組織圖不只可讓教師評鑑學生是否達到教學成效，也能讓學生自我評量其學習成效，為一相當有效的評鑑工具。

電子朗讀音檔下載

請先輸入網址或掃描 QR code 進入「三民．東大音檔網」
https://elearning.sanmin.com.tw/Voice/

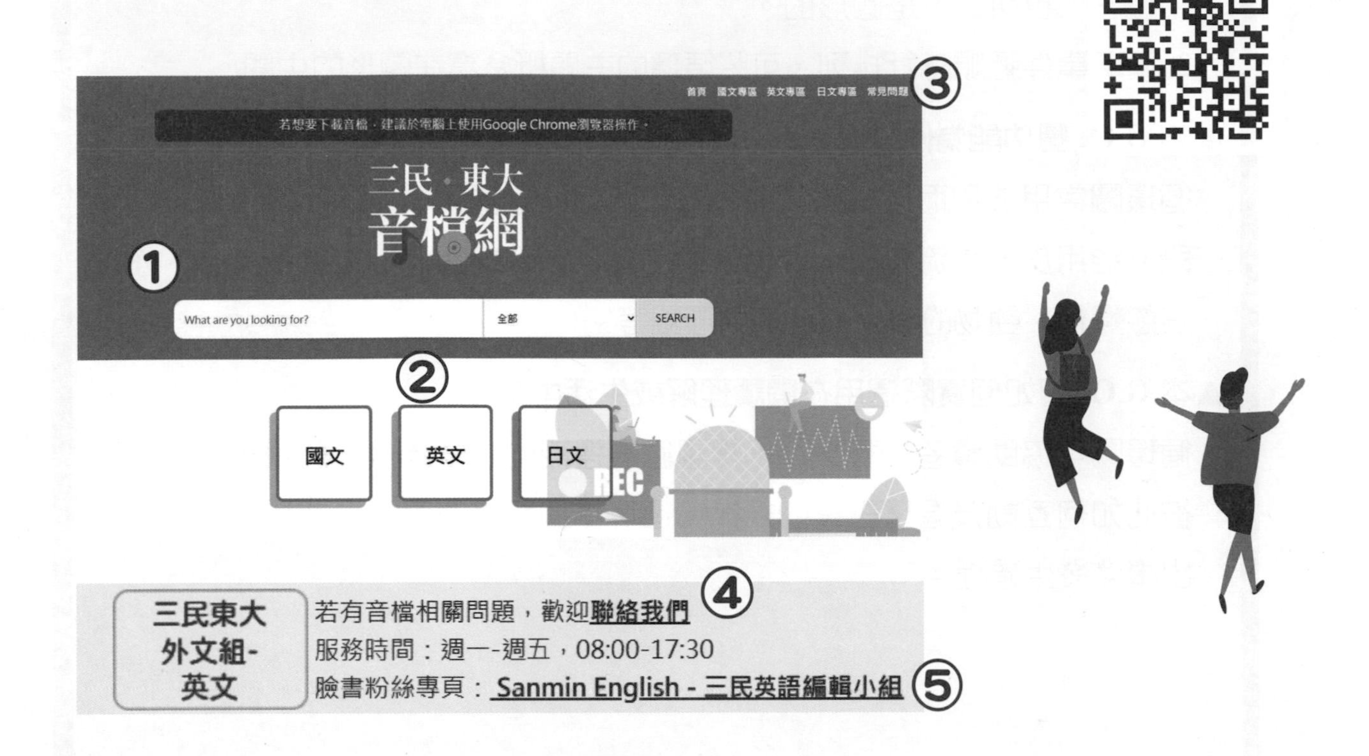

① 輸入本書書名即可找到音檔。請再依提示下載音檔。
② 也可點擊「英文」進入英文專區查找音檔後下載。
③ 若無法順利下載音檔，可至「常見問題」查看相關問題。
④ 若有音檔相關問題，請點擊「聯絡我們」，將盡快為你處理。
⑤ 更多英文新知都在臉書粉絲專頁。

常見的圖形組織圖種類

1 Cycle 循環圖

▲本 G.O. 圖包含什麼元素？

1. 循環圖通常是圓形的，沒有開頭也沒有結尾。但只要能表達循環重複的概念，也可以不是圓形的。
2. 循環事件應順時針排列，可將循環的主題概念寫在圖形的中間。

▲本 G.O. 圖功能為何？

循環圖常用於周而復始的週期，按照固定模式重複發生的步驟、動作或階段。能用於各種流程或一連串發生的事件，例如：月球盈虧的週期、水的三態變化、動物的一生、經濟循環圖等。

▲本 G.O. 圖如何實際運用在閱讀理解或生活中？

循環圖可協助讀者分析文章，辨認循環週期的主要事件，並找出連續事件彼此如何互動及循環重複的規律。也可重述發生的事件，或按照循環圖寫出事件發生過程。

示意圖

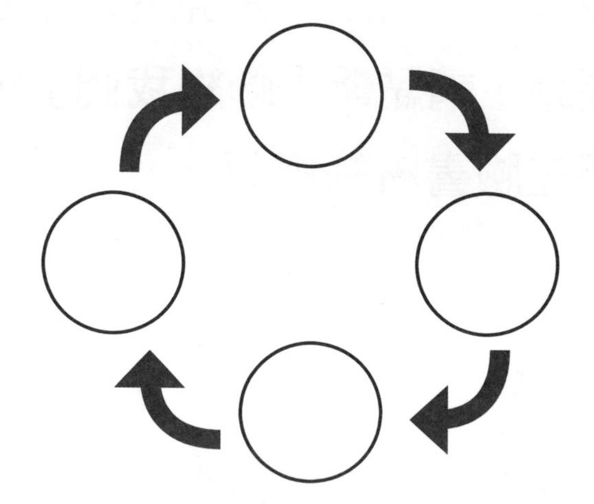

2 Timeline 時間線

▲本 G.O. 圖包含什麼元素？

時間線是將連續發生的事件，按時間順序，放在同一條時間軸上，時間軸上以事件發生的年代或日期來標示。

▲本 G.O. 圖功能為何？

1. 時間線經常用於討論特別的歷史時代、重要歷史事件、某件事物 (音樂、畫派、服裝、建築等) 的發展、人物傳記、日常行程表、科學觀察、計畫時間表等。
2. 時間線也可用在故事的大綱，從故事開始，到最精彩的高潮部分，將發生的重要事件按時間順序排列。

▲本 G.O. 圖如何實際運用在閱讀理解或生活中？

在閱讀以特定歷史事件為背景的故事時，時間線有助於了解此事件，甚至作者對此事件的看法及態度。

示意圖

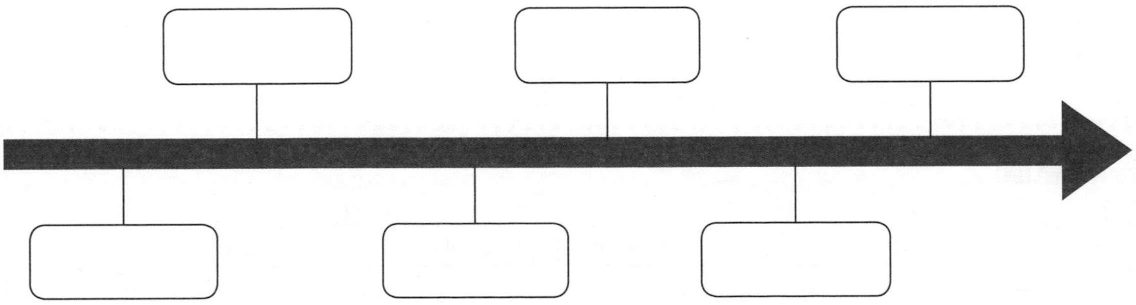

本 G.O. 圖可搭配本書 Unit 1 練習喔！

3 Sequence Chart 循序圖

▲本 G.O. 圖包含什麼元素？

循序圖是由有明確開端與結尾的連續事件所構成。

▲本 G.O. 圖功能為何？

1. 循序圖與循環圖 (Cycle) 的差別在於，循環圖並沒有明確的開始與結尾。
2. 循序圖與時間線 (Timeline) 的差別在於，時間線多用於歷史事件，而循序圖則多用於過程中的階段或步驟。

▲本 G.O. 圖如何實際運用在閱讀理解或生活中？

循序圖包括事件流程圖 (Chain-of-Events or Flowchart)，問題與解決法圖 (Problem-Solution Charts)，因果圖 (Cause-Effect Charts) 三種。

1. 事件流程圖：

   可練習排列事件各階段的順序，用以組織或解釋事件，也可用於描述程序的先後。

2. 問題與解決法圖：

   可用於教師解釋完一個事件或行動後的分組討論。學生可先利用此種組織圖描述或預測問題，然後腦力激盪出各種可能的解決法，及各解決法可能帶來的結果。

3. 因果圖：

   循序圖最常用於表示因果關係，可用於分辨事件的因果，也可用於探討某原因造成的結果，而此結果又可能為原因，並造成另一種結果的線性連鎖關係。

示意圖

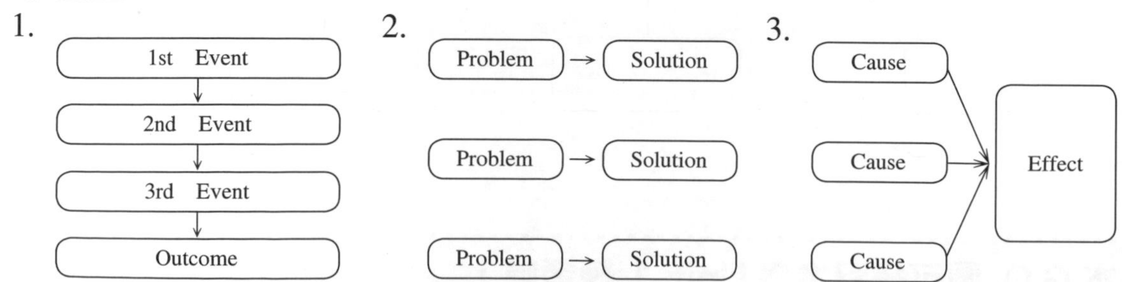

本 G.O. 圖可搭配本書 Unit 2 練習喔！

4 KWL KWL 表

▲本 G.O. 圖包含什麼元素？

KWL 表是由 K、W、L 三個欄位構成的表格：

1. K 代表我知道什麼 (What I Know)：閱讀前，先確認對主題了解多少。
2. W 代表我想知道什麼 (What I Want to Know)：讀者想從閱讀中了解什麼。
3. L 代表我學到了什麼 (What I Learned)：閱讀後學到 W 欄位想知道的答案。

▲本 G.O. 圖功能為何？

KWL 表填表時，心理會經過連結 (Making Associations)、預測 (Predicting)、產生問題 (Generating Questions)、澄清 (Clarifying)、摘要 (Summarizing)、評鑑 (Evaluating) 等過程，可提升閱讀能力。

▲本 G.O. 圖如何實際運用在閱讀理解或生活中？

1. KWL 表可延伸為以下幾種：

(1) K-W-H-L：除了本來的 KWL 表格外，還要去思考如何學習到想學的東西 (How I will learn what I want to learn)。

(2) K-W-L-W-H：完成 KWL 表格後，可繼續回答：

① 關於主題還想學什麼 (What else I want to learn about the topic)

② 如何找到這些資料 (How I will find that information)

(3) K-W-L-H：完成 KWL 表後，增加了 H，代表我們如何學到更多 (How I can learn more)，要如何找到跟主題相關的其他額外的資訊。

(4) K-W-L-Q：完成 KWL 表後，增加提問 (Questions)，鼓勵提出更多的問題，持續探究、記錄與分析資料，做出成果報告。

2. KWL 表可用於任何領域的課程，大大提升閱讀能力。

示意圖

Topic:		
What I Know	What I Want to Know	What I Learned

本 G.O. 圖可搭配本書 Unit 3 練習喔！

5 Flowchart 流程圖

▲本 G.O. 圖包含什麼元素？

流程圖用特定的圖形、符號來表達解決問題的順序和步驟。常用的符號如下：

1. 橢圓形、圓角矩形、圓形：表示任何具有開始和結束活動的進程。
2. 矩形：表示進程活動或步驟。
3. 菱形：在做出決定或要回答的問題時使用，如「是、否」或「真、假」。
4. 箭頭線：路徑，表示流程進行方向，用於顯示從一個步驟到另一個步驟的操作流程。它們也表示從一步到另一步的進展。
5. 平行四邊形：用於表示輸入、輸出。

▲本 G.O. 圖功能為何？

流程圖將解決問題的順序、步驟，用特定的圖形、符號表達出來。為了方便流通閱讀，每個符號都有其特殊意義，而且符號必須是固定且前後一致的。

▲本 G.O. 圖如何實際運用在閱讀理解或生活中？

流程圖用於閱讀的文本時，一般並無複雜的流程，通常只有始點→處理程序→終點。但日常生活中流程圖較為複雜，可分為：

1. 文件流程圖：用以表示整個系統的文件流程。
2. 資料流程圖：用以表示整個系統的資料流程。
3. 系統流程圖：用以表示實際資源操作的流程。
4. 程式流程圖：用以表示系統內程式控制的流程。

示意圖

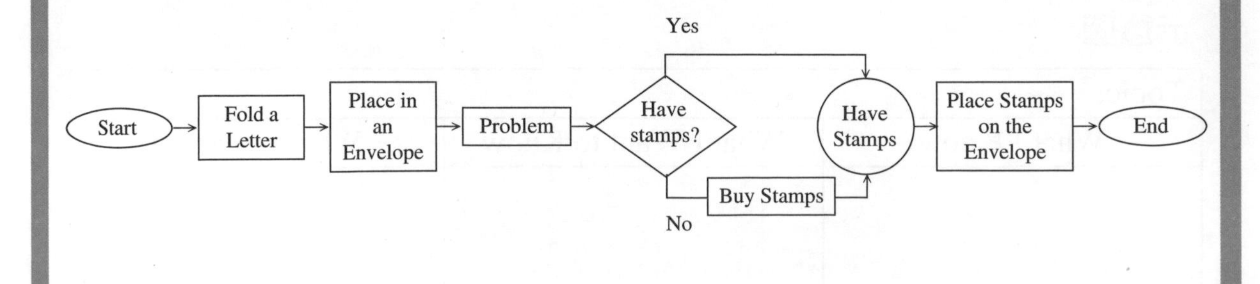

6 Star Diagram 星形圖

▲本 G.O. 圖包含什麼元素？

星形圖呈現只有單一主題，卻有多項相關的概念、事實或屬性的內容。

▲本 G.O. 圖功能為何？

1. 星形圖是將想法圖像化的組織圖，由圈圈與圈圈的連結，可看出主題與延伸概念的關聯性。
2. 網狀圖 (Webbing Diagram) 和群集圖 (Cluster Diagram) 兩者，與星形圖 (Star Diagram) 一樣，都有呈現與單一主題相關概念內容的功能。

▲本 G.O. 圖如何實際運用在閱讀理解或生活中？

1. 星形圖、網狀圖、或群集圖可用於寫作前腦力激盪的情境中，以找出與主題相關的事項。以下為兩種建議運用方式：
   (1) 根據中心主題腦力激盪出所有想得到的點子，再將這些衍生的點子按從屬關係或不同屬性分開歸類及排序 (Clustering and Ordering)。就點子間的關係，根據其從屬關係或階層關係進行分類，就完成一個群集圖。
   (2) 在一張空白紙中畫一圓圈，並於其中寫上主題；將任何與主題相關的點子寫在主題圓圈周圍的圓圈：將這些與新主題相關的點子以線與主題圓圈相連；根據每個新點子，再想一些相關點子在其周圍的圓圈中，並以線連接；完成後，其中最多圓圈連接的就是最可能的主題。
2. 星形圖、網狀圖、或群集圖也可用於回想閱讀完的內容，分類或總結作為複習及加深記憶的輔助。

示意圖

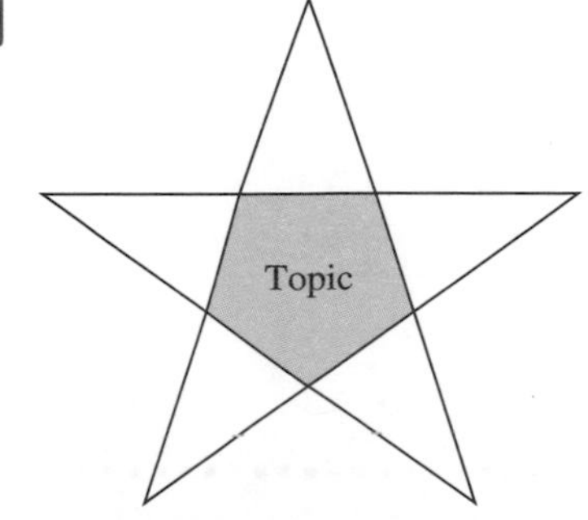

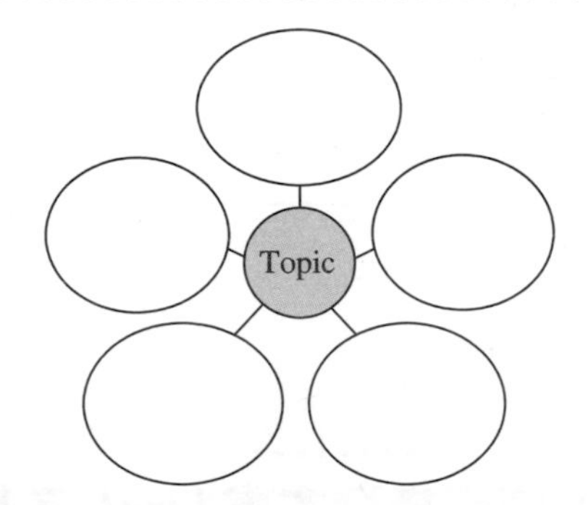

本 G.O. 圖可搭配本書 Unit 4 練習喔！

7 Spider Diagram 蜘蛛圖

▲本 G.O. 圖包含什麼元素？

蜘蛛圖以圖片或字為中心，而由中心放射延伸出來的數隻「腳」，為中心概念的數個面向。每個面向為中心概念的次概念，每隻「腳」上，須再添加幾個次概念下的次次概念。

▲本 G.O. 圖功能為何？

蜘蛛圖主要是以視覺的方式將概念有邏輯地排列，主要用於寫作前的計畫、創造或激發靈感。可用來腦力激盪虛構故事中的角色特性，也可用來收集資料、分門別類。

▲本 G.O. 圖如何實際運用在閱讀理解或生活中？

在閱讀一般文本，或處理生活中的資訊時，都適合以蜘蛛圖快速簡單地整理複雜的概念與點子，而這種資料分類的模式，也是最接近人類腦部的運作方式。

示意圖

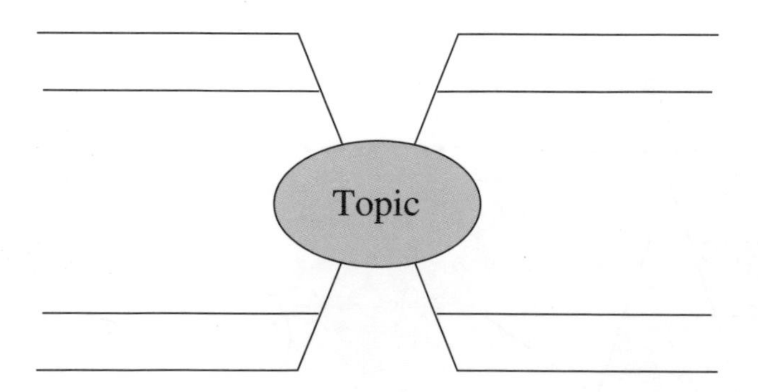

本 G.O. 圖可搭配本書 Unit 5 練習喔！

8 Fishbone Diagram 魚骨圖

▲本 G.O. 圖包含什麼元素？

1. 魚骨圖，又稱特性要因圖、因果分析圖、石川圖 (Ishikawa Diagram)，是由日本學者石川馨先生所發展出來的。
2. 魚骨圖包含魚頭以及骨頭，以下為各部位呈現的內容：
   (1) 在確定要討論的主題後，先在魚頭上寫出待解決的問題，進行腦力激盪。
   (2) 將找出的因素歸類、整理，並確定其從屬關係。將因素分為主要原因、次要原因、或是更次要的小因素。
   (3) 將主要原因衍生出的次要原因，寫在大骨分出來的中骨上，接著繼續找出小因素，將之寫在中骨分出來的小骨上，以此找出最關鍵的因素。

▲本 G.O. 圖功能為何？

魚骨圖是一種發現問題根本原因的方法。不管是規劃活動流程、分析問題、製作專案等等，都可以使用。

▲本 G.O. 圖如何實際運用在閱讀理解或生活中？

1. 魚骨圖可用於因果文寫作前的腦力激盪，或因果文閱讀後的架構分析。
2. 魚骨圖也常被用於質量改善分析、人事管理、制定作業標準等。

示意圖

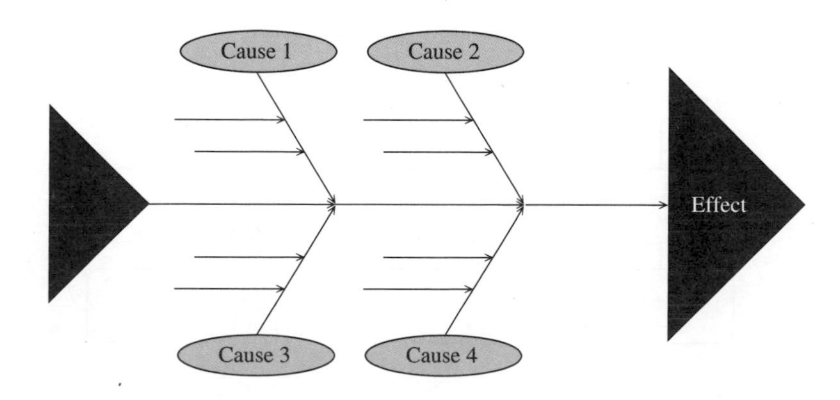

本 G.O. 圖可搭配本書 Unit 6 練習喔！

9 Tree Diagram 樹狀圖

▲本 G.O. 圖包含什麼元素？

1. 樹狀圖是與家庭樹相同概念的組織圖，第一層樹幹代表主題，第二層樹枝代表相關的事實、因素、影響、特色、結果等，依此再往下列出第三層、第四層等支持細節。
2. 像小樹長成大樹一樣，樹狀圖為向下延伸的放射性思考，唯上下顛倒，根在上方，樹葉在下方。

▲本 G.O. 圖功能為何？

1. 樹狀圖常用於分類與組織資料，尤其適合邏輯分析。
2. 閱讀時，樹狀圖可幫助了解主旨及回想文中元素間的關係。
3. 寫作時，樹狀圖也有助於組織概念，讓文章有層次感。

▲本 G.O. 圖如何實際運用在閱讀理解或生活中？

1. 幾乎所有學科都可利用樹狀圖來做分析，例如：英文句法分析、數學機率分析。
2. 樹狀圖可用來分類，例如：英文動詞的分類、動物分類等。
3. 樹狀圖也用來推敲原因，例如：令顧客滿意的要素，或是預測結果，例如：全球暖化可能造成的後果等。

示意圖

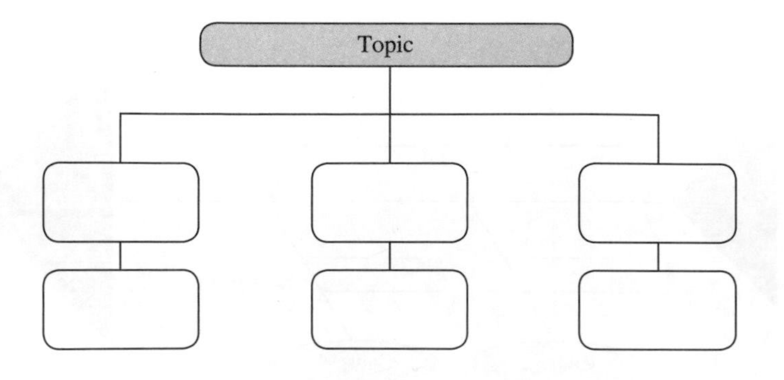

本 G.O. 圖可搭配本書 Unit 7 練習喔！

10 T-Chart T 形圖

▲本 G.O. 圖包含什麼元素？

T 形圖是一個 T 字組成的圖表，主要用來區分兩種不同的事物或情況，常用於分析比較一個情況或事件的兩面。

▲本 G.O. 圖功能為何？

T 形圖於閱讀或寫作說明文時，可用於分析優點與缺點、問題與解決法、事實與意見、相同與相異之處等。

▲本 G.O. 圖如何實際運用在閱讀理解或生活中？

1. T 形圖可用於閱讀故事時，分析故事中歷史真實與虛構的部分，也可比較兩個不同的角色。於比較完成後，再根據 T 形圖內容進行討論。
2. T 形圖也可用於其他學科，如於社會學科中，討論某一政策錯誤與改正的要點。
3. 在日常生活中，T 形圖也經常被使用，例如：做決定前，可討論該做 (Dos) 與不該做 (Don'ts) 的事。

示意圖

A	B

本 G.O. 圖可搭配本書 Unit 8 練習喔！

11 Venn Diagram 文氏圖 (維恩圖)

▲本 G.O. 圖包含什麼元素？

文氏圖一般由兩個圓圈部分重疊而成，主要用來比較與對比兩個事物相同與相異之處，中間重疊的部分為相同之處，兩旁不重疊的部分為相異之處。也可以三圈、四圈或更多圈圈來對比。

▲本 G.O. 圖功能為何？

抽象的概念或複雜的關係可以透過文氏圖比較與對比將其視覺化，以釐清思考的方向，也可引發討論。

▲本 G.O. 圖如何實際運用在閱讀理解或生活中？

1. 文氏圖用於閱讀與寫作時，可比較與對比兩個角色、物件、動物、國家、選擇、制度等，例如：比較與對比虛構的故事與寫實文學，或比較與對比昆蟲與鳥類等。
2. 文氏圖最初運用在數學，尤其是計數問題，文氏圖可清楚地輔助我們對於集合概念的理解，例如：一個 30 人的班級，有 10 個人喜歡貓，14 個人喜歡狗，7 個人喜歡貓也喜歡狗，請問有幾人不喜歡貓也不喜歡狗？畫出文氏圖，答案即呼之欲出。

示意圖

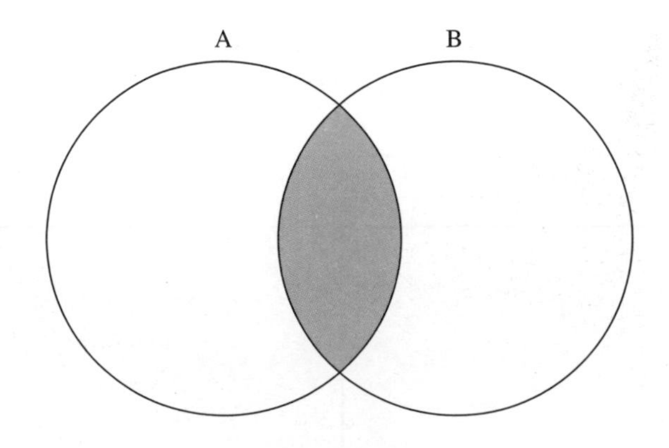

本 G.O. 圖可搭配本書 Unit 9 練習喔！

12 Sandwich (Hamburger) Chart 三明治 (漢堡) 圖

▲本 G.O. 圖包含什麼元素？

1. 三明治圖又稱為漢堡圖，是由兩片吐司或漢堡麵包組成。
2. 頂層麵包是吸引讀者注意的主題，底層麵包則為文章總結。
3. 而中間夾的漢堡肉、生菜和起司為支持細節，一般為三個觀點：事實、例子、理由等，用以支持文章主旨。

▲本 G.O. 圖功能為何？

三明治圖能協助讀者組織想法，找出文本的概念或想法及其組織與結構，具體呈現訊息間的關係。

▲本 G.O. 圖如何實際運用在閱讀理解或生活中？

1. 三明治圖通常用於寫作前的腦力激盪，按照此組織圖思考，能輕鬆寫出內容充實豐滿又結構嚴謹的文章。
2. 三明治圖也可用來分析自己的文章，填入三明治圖中，能清楚看出文章哪個部分不足，可即時補足，並重新安排組織架構，讓內容更豐富、順暢、合邏輯。

示意圖

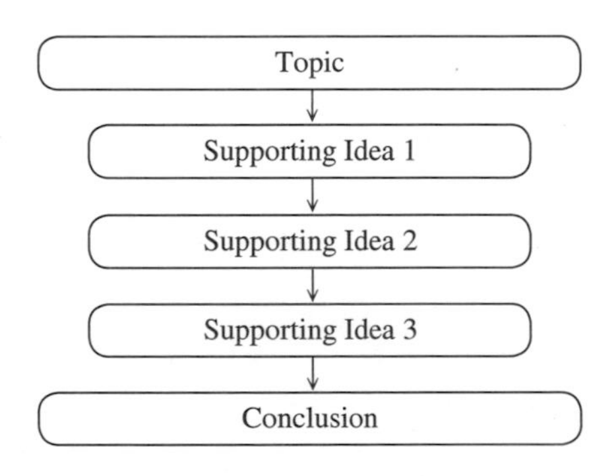

本 G.O. 圖可搭配本書 Unit 10 練習喔！

13 OREO Chart OREO 圖

▲本 G.O. 圖包含什麼元素？

1. OREO 圖與三明治圖及漢堡圖類似，均以熟悉的食物意象來比喻文章的架構。
2. OREO 中的 O 指的是 Opinion 意見，R 指的是 Reason 理由，而 E 為 Example 例子。

▲本 G.O. 圖功能為何？

1. 閱讀後，可利用 OREO 圖，第一段提出意見，中間的段落提出理由，並舉例支持自己的意見，最後一段再次強調自己的意見。
2. 如果有更多的理由支持自己的意見時，可在餅乾中夾雙層、三層或更多餡料，例如：三個理由即可寫成 ORERERE O。

▲本 G.O. 圖如何實際運用在閱讀理解或生活中？

OREO 圖可用於意見討論或辯論。利用 OREO 圖，可在討論或辯論前有邏輯地思考，並整理支持論點的理由且舉出實例，讓意見更站得住腳。

示意圖

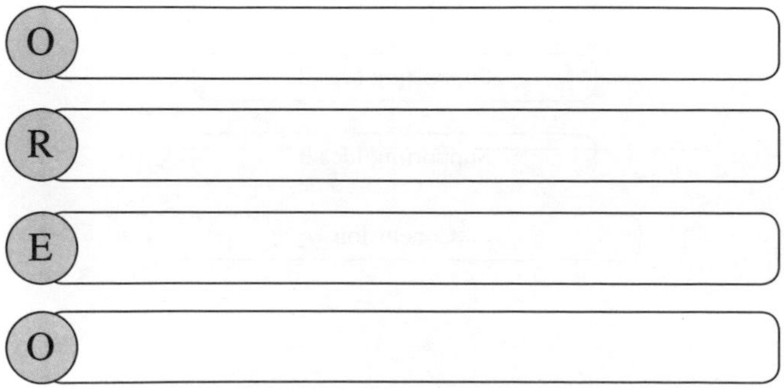

O
R
E
O

14 Story Map: Beginning, Middle, End 故事圖：開頭、中間、結尾

▲本 G.O. 圖包含什麼元素？

1. 故事圖有許多種類與形式，而本圖教學生辨認故事的開頭、中間、結尾，是最簡單的一種故事圖。
2. 開頭部分介紹故事主要的角色、他們的目標、時間和地點，以及主要的問題，故事的氛圍從頭到底應該一致。
3. 中段部分一連串事件發生，增加故事的緊張程度。處理故事衝突時，角色也開始成長轉變，有些小的危機暫時解決，但故事繼續朝高潮的方向發展。
4. 故事結尾時，主要衝突已經解決，緊張局勢很快落幕，直至故事結束。

▲本 G.O. 圖功能為何？

此種故事圖可讓學生簡單地了解故事架構，寫故事時，也能有開頭的鋪陳、中段的高潮，以及合理的結尾。

▲本 G.O. 圖如何實際運用在閱讀理解或生活中？

故事圖不限用於語言學習，也可用於數學，利用故事圖出題，另外也可用於社會學科。

示意圖

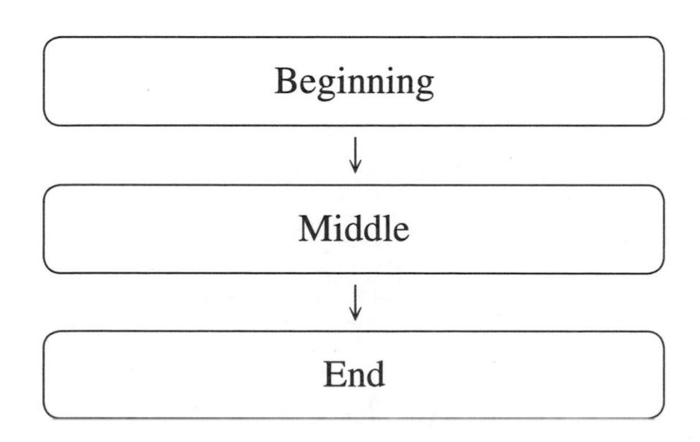

15 Story Map: 5W's 5W 故事圖

▲本 G.O. 圖包含什麼元素？

1. 5W 故事圖是利用五個 wh- 問句來協助讀者更了解故事內容。
2. 5W 分別代表：
   (1) **What** happened? 發生了什麼事？
   (2) **Who** was there? 故事裡有誰？
   (3) **Why** did it happen? 為什麼會發生此事？
   (4) **When** did it happen? 何時發生？
   (5) **Where** did it happen? 在哪裡發生？
3. 此類型圖表，有時還會加上 1H：
   (6) **How** did it happen? 如何發生的？

▲本 G.O. 圖功能為何？

5W 故事圖中的 5W，Who 用於詢問 Characters 角色，When、Where 用於詢問 Setting 情節背景，What、How、Why 用於詢問情節。

▲本 G.O. 圖如何實際運用在閱讀理解或生活中？

1. 提升對故事的了解。
2. 辨認組成故事的要素。
3. 幫助讀者用不同的方式組織資訊及想法。
4. 可全班或分小組進行。
5. 可在閱讀課程中，或閱讀後進行。

示意圖

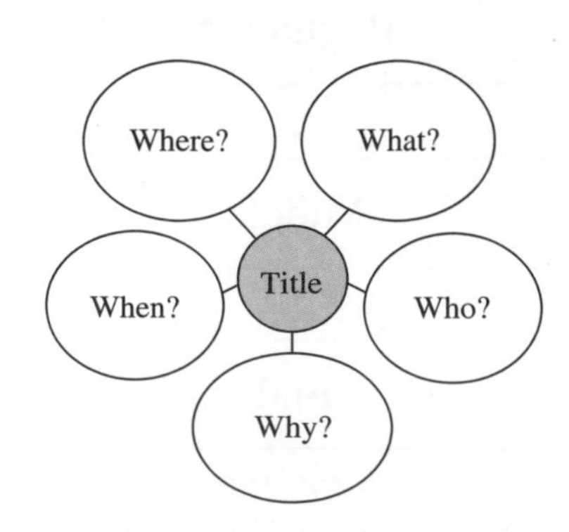

16 Character Traits 角色特色圖

▲本 **G.O.** 圖包含什麼元素？

因應不同的目的，有不同角色特色組織圖：

1. 為更了解故事的主角或數個角色，組織圖可包括角色的：

    (1) 想法 (Thoughts)　(2) 說過的話 (Quotes)　(3) 行為 (Actions)

    (4) 感覺 (Feelings)　(5) 目的 (Goals)　(6) 描述 (Descriptions)

    (7) 其他角色對此角色的看法 (What others say about this)

    (8) 其他值得提的事 (Something else important)

2. 比較分析兩個角色的組織圖：

    (1) 針對各個角色的想法、說過的話、行為、感覺、目的、性格等做比較。

    (2) 比較及對比角色間相同相異之處。

    (3) 比較分析角色對事件或問題的看法。

▲本 **G.O.** 圖功能為何？

1. 使讀者更了解故事中的角色。
2. 讓讀者分析角色的改變。
3. 使讀者更了解角色對問題的看法及感想。
4. 讓讀者比較故事中的角色。

▲本 **G.O.** 圖如何實際運用在閱讀理解或生活中？

1. 藉角色分析深入了解其動機，讀者可更清楚故事情節的細微變化，也讓閱讀更有趣。
2. 讀者可練習批判性思考，有效地分析角色。

示意圖

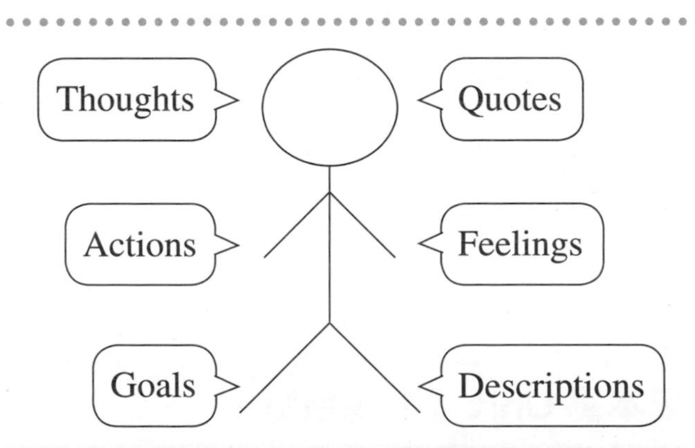

17 Honeycomb Story Map 蜂巢故事圖

▲本 G.O. 圖包含什麼元素？

蜂巢故事圖因像蜂巢而得名，通常少則由五個或七個六角形組成，當然也可以更多。每個蜂巢所代表的元素因文體不同而有差異。

▲本 G.O. 圖功能為何？

1. 蜂巢故事圖以不等數目的六角形蜂巢以線性或環狀方式組合，除更能顯現元素間的緊密關係外，也能利用其環狀特色凸顯核心元素。
2. 蜂巢故事圖常用於分析故事，或協助讀者練習寫故事，例如：五格蜂巢可用分別是時間、地點、角色、問題與解決法，七格蜂巢可由標題 (Title)、人物 (Who)、地點 (Where)、時間 (When)、目的 (What)、原因 (Why)，以及寓意 (Message) 組成。

▲本 G.O. 圖如何實際運用在閱讀理解或生活中？

蜂巢圖除了用於故事分析，也可用於分析說明文，例如：將結果置於中間，原因環列四周；或主旨置於中間，例子列於四周；或問題置於中間，可能的解決法放在四周。此時蜂巢圖與花形組織圖用法及功能相同。

示意圖

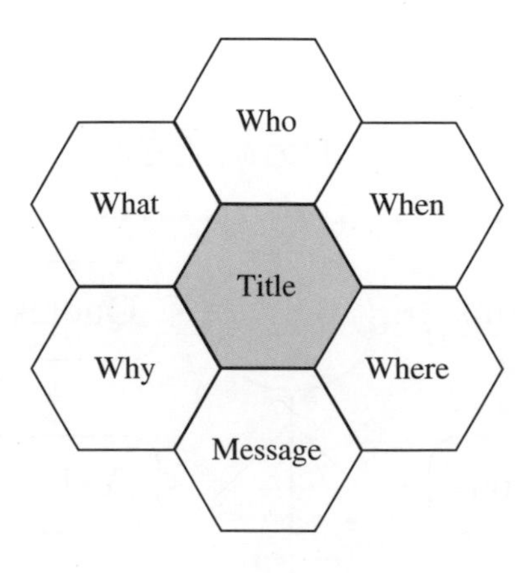

本 G.O. 圖可搭配本書 Unit 11 練習喔！

18 Story Mountain 故事山峰圖

▲本 G.O. 圖包含什麼元素？

1. 故事山峰圖是根據故事發展的模式，由開頭發展到發現問題，再發展到故事的最高潮，然後問題獲得解決，故事也急轉直下直到結束。
2. 故事山峰圖由以下的元素組成：

(1) 故事開頭 (Beginning or Exposition)：包含背景資料 (Background Information)、角色 (Characters) 及場景 (Setting)。

(2) 情節鋪陳 (Rising Action)：主角採取行動去解決問題，通常包含數個連續發生的事件，也可能面臨突發狀況或轉折 (Twist)。此階段還包含問題與衝突 (Conflict)，主角面臨的問題，可分為外部衝突 (External Conflict) 與內部衝突 (Internal Conflict)，前者指故事角色與外部因素的衝突，後者指故事角色自身性格的衝突。

(3) 高潮 (Climax)：故事高潮通常發生在問題即將獲得解決時，讀者或許無法得知故事如何完結，但卻知問題必會解決，且高潮與衝突必定是相關的。

(4) 劇情收尾 (Falling Action)：故事高潮過後，讀者知道衝突解決後會發生什麼，劇情一般也會急轉直下直到結尾。

(5) 結局 (Resolution)：讓讀者知道衝突獲得解決後，主角會有怎樣的結局。有時也會解釋一些較小未解的懸疑，也可能留下部分懸疑自行猜測。

▲本 G.O. 圖功能為何？

1. 故事山峰圖主要用來分析記敘文，將故事的發展情節作階段性的拆解。
2. 故事山峰圖可增加讀者對故事的了解，分析情節的起承轉合。

▲本 G.O. 圖如何實際運用在閱讀理解或生活中？

除了分析文本，讀者亦可利用故事山峰圖，先擬出大綱，進而寫出有衝突、有高潮，引人入勝的故事。

示意圖

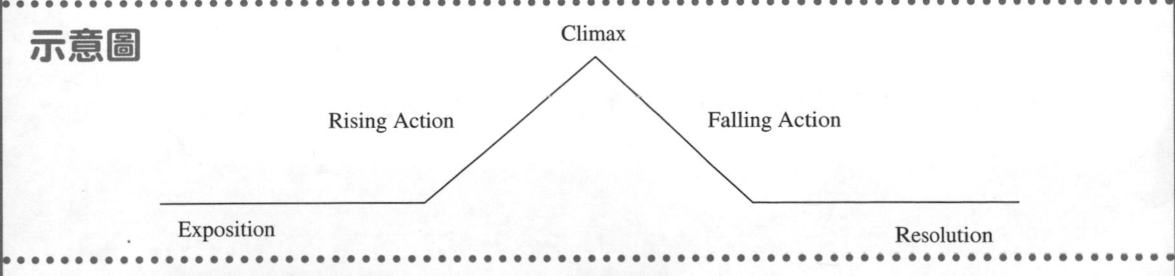

本 G.O. 圖可搭配本書 Unit 12 練習喔！

G.O.,G.O.,G.O.! 規則說明

Let's Go

鯨魚是海洋中的大型哺乳類動物，然而碩大的體型並不能保證牠們的安全，有什麼原因會造成鯨魚擱淺、死亡呢？本單元 G.O. 圖搭配 Fishbone Diagram (魚骨圖) 學習，以下為 Fishbone Diagram 的說明以及示意圖。

說明	示意圖
1. 魚骨圖包含魚頭及身體骨頭，常用在因果分析。 2. 魚頭為問題或結果，身體的骨頭則為導致此問題或結果的因素。 3. 依據因素的層級，大骨頭表示主要原因，次要以及更次要的原因，則分別列在中骨頭及小骨頭上。	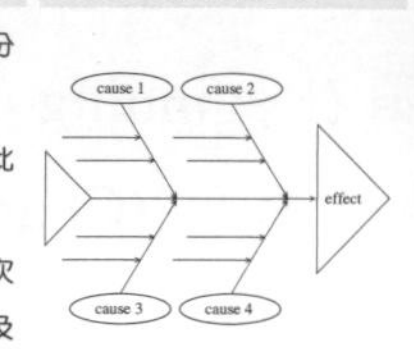

- 每課從課文大意起跑，裝備上 G.O. 圖說明及示意圖。
- 初步了解課文。Let's Go!

Animal testing has long been a **controversial issue**. On the one hand, it **contributes** to medical breakthroughs that could greatly benefit mankind, but on the other hand, it comes at the expense of

- 跑道中段為每課課文，單字、片語、認讀字都是課文內的風景。
- 每課單字為精壯的粗體，與片語、認讀字站在頁面右側。
- 每課片語穿上粉紅色衣服，與單字、認讀字站在頁面右側。
- 每課認讀字身著綠色衣服，與單字、片語一起站在頁面右側。

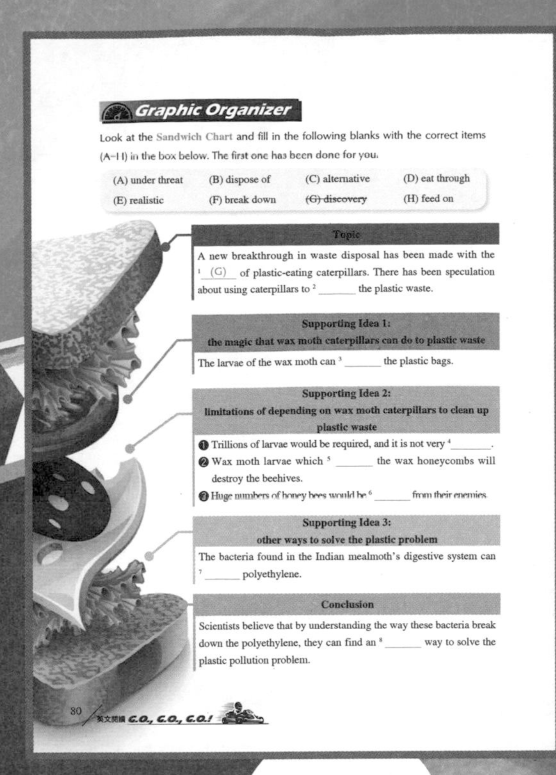

Graphic Organizer

Look at the Sandwich Chart and fill in the following blanks with the correct items (A–H) in the box below. The first one has been done for you.

(A) under threat (B) dispose of (C) alternative (D) eat through
(E) realistic (F) break down ~~(G) discovery~~ (H) feed on

Topic
A new breakthrough in waste disposal has been made with the [1] (G) of plastic-eating caterpillars. There has been speculation about using caterpillars to [2] ______ the plastic waste.

Supporting Idea 1:
the magic that wax moth caterpillars can do to plastic waste
The larvae of the wax moth can [3] ______ the plastic bags.

Supporting Idea 2:
limitations of depending on wax moth caterpillars to clean up plastic waste
❶ Trillions of larvae would be required, and it is not very [4] ______.
❷ Wax moth larvae which [5] ______ the wax honeycombs will destroy the beehives.
❸ Huge numbers of honey bees would be [6] ______ from their enemies.

Supporting Idea 3:
other ways to solve the plastic problem
The bacteria found in the Indian mealmoth's digestive system can [7] ______ polyethylene.

Conclusion
Scientists believe that by understanding the way these bacteria break down the polyethylene, they can find an [8] ______ way to solve the plastic pollution problem.

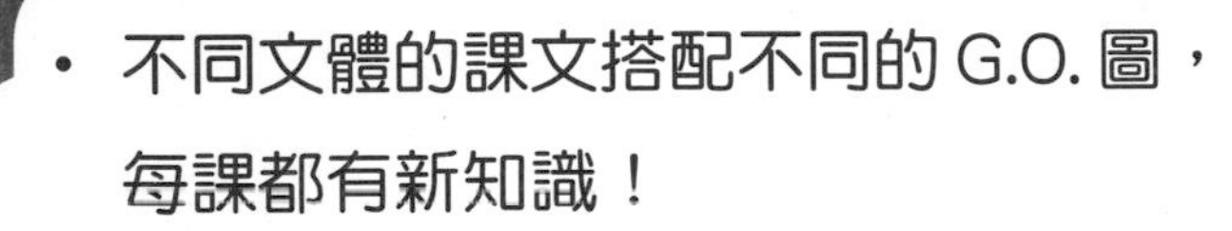

- 不同文體的課文搭配不同的 G.O. 圖，每課都有新知識！
- 最終衝刺前，用 G.O. 圖幫你釐清思緒。衝向終點 G.O.,G.O.,G.O.!

Reading Comprehension

According to the passage and the following instructions, answer the questions below.

(　　) 1. Which of the following pictures best describes the third paragraph?

擷取訊息 (A)

(B)

(C)

(D)

(　　) 2. What was the four guests' first reaction to Dr. Heidegger's experiment?

擷取訊息 (A) They looked forward to it.
(B) They didn't expect it to work.
(C) They couldn't wait to try it.
(D) They drank the liquid without delay.

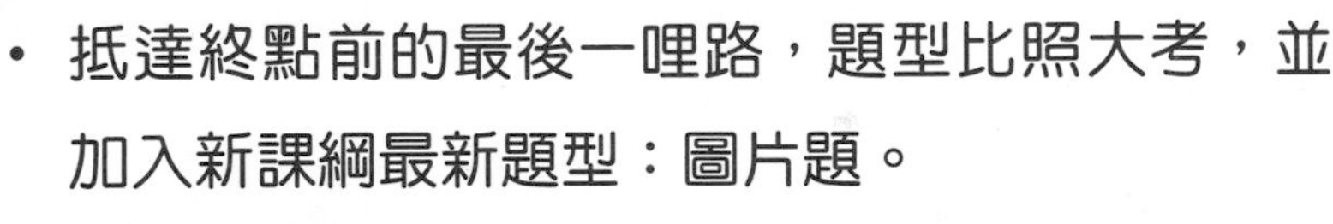

- 抵達終點前的最後一哩路，題型比照大考，並加入新課綱最新題型：圖片題。
- 符合新課綱 111 學年度大考測驗題型之標準。
- 標記測驗重點，檢視你的學習成效！
- G.O.,G.O.,G.O.! 抵達終點！

G.O.,G.O.,G.O.!
抵達終點！

CONTENTS

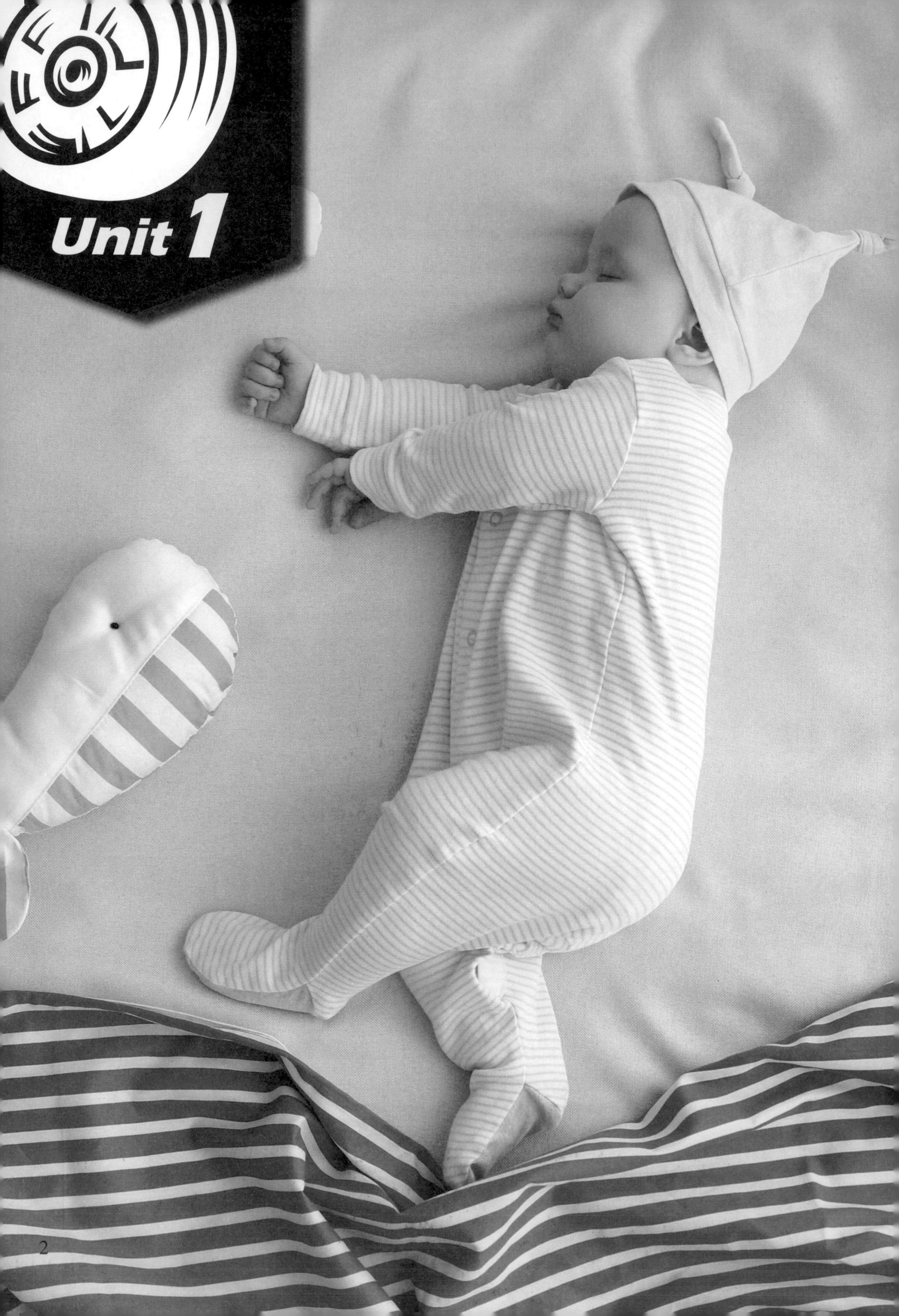
Unit 1

How We Used to **Sleep**

Let's Go

睡眠在我們生活中扮演極為重要的角色。本單元談論人類的睡眠歷史，藉由觀察不同時期床鋪型態的演進，得知睡眠在人類進化過程中的重要性。本單元 G.O. 圖搭配 **Timeline (時間線)** 學習，以下為 **Timeline** 的說明以及示意圖。

說明	示意圖
1. 時間線將連續發生的事件，按時間先後順序，放在同一條時間軸上，讓讀者能了解事件發展的脈絡，排序文章的重要訊息。 2. 時間線常用在敘述文中。藉由事件的排序，讓讀者釐清事件前後脈絡。讀者可利用時間線分析重要歷史事件、某事物的發展、人物傳記、科學觀察、行程計畫時間表等。	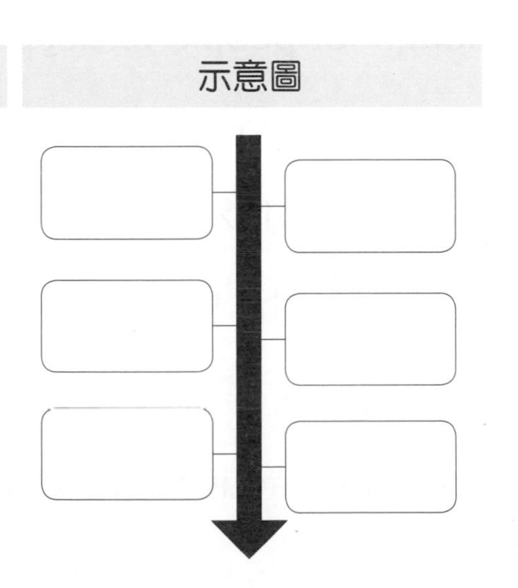

❶ Studies have shown we don't get enough quality sleep. It is not surprising really. Our lives are stressful and we modern people often stay up too late. **Contrary** to the common **notion** that people in the past led hard but more balanced lives, historically people didn't really sleep much better than we do now.

❷ The earliest known beds were made around 8000 B.C. The so-called beds were simply grass and soft flora stuffed in small hollows along the walls of caves. Actually, these beds were only big enough for people to sleep in the fetal position. They were certainly not the type you find in 5-star **accommodation**.

❸ As civilization advanced, things didn't get much better sleep-wise. The Romans treated the necessity for sleep with a kind of contempt, as it took up time that could have been **devoted** to more **productive** activities, like building roads or bridges. The Romans

preferred to sleep on small wooden-**framed** beds with mattresses stuffed with straw in humble plain rooms, waking up long before dawn. 15

❹ Sleep quality seems to have gotten worse in the Middle Ages. Most **notably**, it was the smell that was almost intolerable. Back then, people lacked proper sewage systems, lived in unsanitary conditions, and constantly had fires burning. The smell of feces, sweat, and smoke must have been foul indeed. In addition, families tended to sleep huddled together to keep warm, so there was very little privacy. 20 25

Words for Production

1. contrary *adj.* 相反的
2. notion *n.* [C] 觀念
3. accommodation *n.* [U] 住處
4. devote *vt.* 用於，致力於
5. productive *adj.* 有效益的
6. framed *adj.* 外框的
7. notably *adv.* 尤其，特別

Idioms and Phrases

1. take up something 佔用 (時間)

Words for Recognition

1. flora *n.* [U] 植物群
2. fetal *adj.* 像胎兒一樣的
3. contempt *n.* [U] 輕視，蔑視
4. mattress *n.* [C] 床墊
5. the Middle Ages *n. pl.* 中世紀
6. sewage *n.* [U] 汙水
7. unsanitary *adj.* 不衛生的，不潔的
8. feces *n. pl.* (*fml.*) 糞便
9. foul *adj.* 惡臭難聞的
10. huddle *vi.* (因寒冷或害怕) 擠在一起

❺ The Renaissance is when people's quality of sleep started to improve. People of this period stretched ropes across bed frames to support mattresses and make beds less **rigid**. At the same time in China, during the Ming dynasty, large decorative bed frames were crafted. These pretty beds were not only for sleeping in, but also for entertaining guests during the daytime.

❻ The **invention** of **artificial** light in the Industrial Revolution dramatically changed the way people slept. Before the Industrial Revolution, people would wake up in the middle of the night after about four hours of sleep to do chores and then go back to bed for another four hours. With the invention of the light bulb, people

didn't need to go to sleep right after sunset. 40
Instead, they began to stay up late and hang out with friends. It was not until the 1920s that people adopted an uninterrupted 8-hour sleeping pattern. In recent years, sleep researchers have recommended eight hours 45
of sleep for the sake of our health.

❼ Even though we don't have the healthiest sleeping habits, at least most of us still have a roof over our heads, and a warm comfortable bed to sleep in at night. 50

Words for Production

8. rigid *adj.* 僵硬、僵直的
9. invention *n.* [U] 發明
10. artificial *adj.* 人工的

Idioms and Phrases

2. hang out 閒晃，遊蕩
3. for the sake of 因為…的緣故
4. at least 至少

Words for Recognition

11. the Renaissance *n. sing.* 文藝復興時期 (14–16 世紀)
12. craft *vt.* (尤指用手工) 精心製作
13. the Industrial Revolution *n. sing.* 工業革命 (18–19 世紀)
14. uninterrupted *adj.* 不間斷的

Graphic Organizer

Look at the **Timeline** and fill in the following blanks with the correct items (A–F) in the box below. The first one has been done for you.

(A) The Romans treated the necessity for sleep with a kind of contempt.

(B) the Renaissance (14–16 A.D.)

(C) Most of people have a comfortable bed to sleep in.

(D) Families slept huddled together, so there was little privacy.

~~(E) The beds were only big enough for people to sleep in the fetal position.~~

(F) the Industrial Revolution (18–19 A.D.)

8000 B.C.

- The earliest known beds were made.
- The hollows were stuffed with grass and soft flora.
- 1 (E)

Civilization advanced

- 2 ______
- People slept on small wooden-framed beds with mattresses stuffed with straw.

the Middle Ages

- The quality of sleep got worse.
- The smell was intolerable.
- 3 ______

4 ______ & the Ming dynasty

- The quality of sleep started to improve.
- Decorative bed frames were used.

5 ______

- Artificial light changed the way people slept.

Nowadays

- Sleeping habits are not the healthiest.
- 6 ______

Reading Comprehension

According to the passage and the following instructions, answer the questions below.

(　　) 1. Which of the following pictures is most likely to be bed from 10,000 years

擷取訊息 ago?

(A) 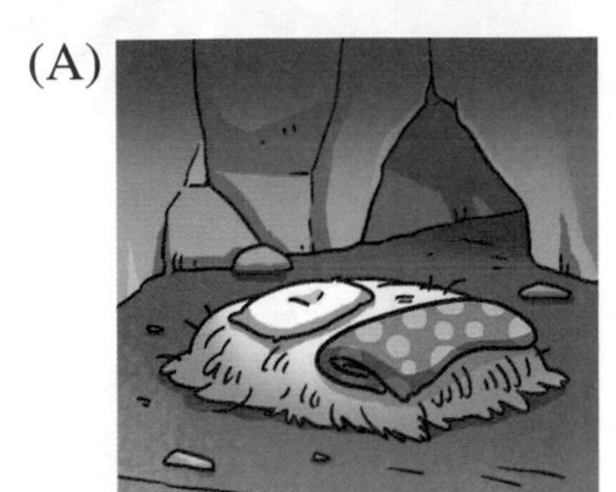

(B) 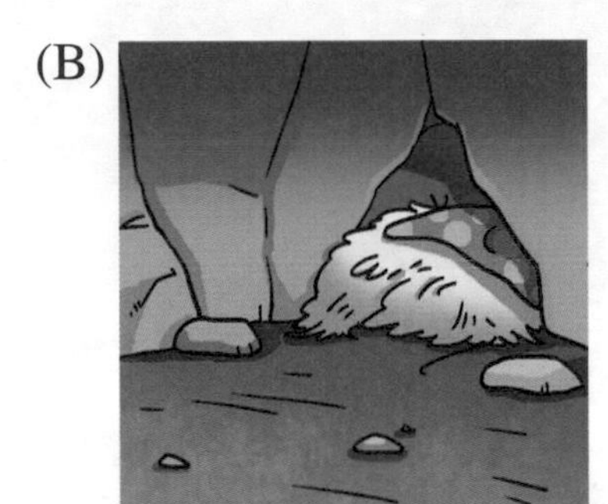

(C) 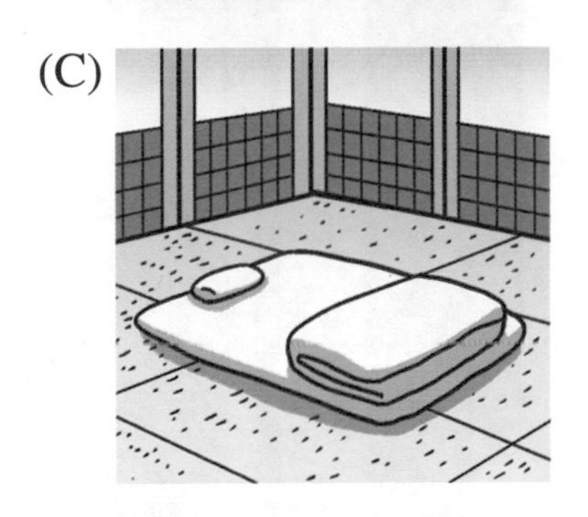

(D) 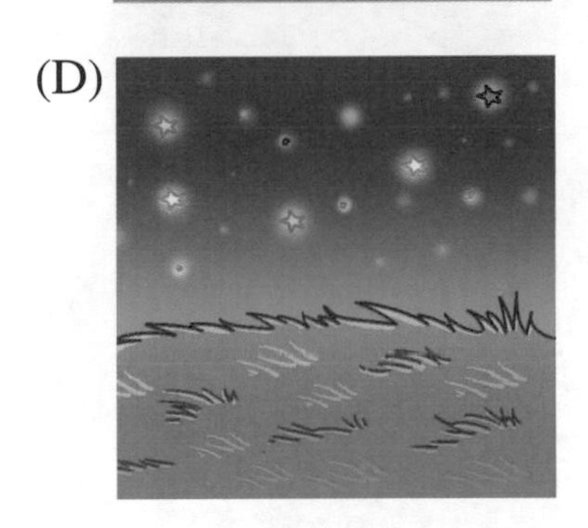

(　　) 2. What is the passage mainly about?

推論整合 (A) How people considered sleeping.

(B) What beds were made of.

(C) Why people did not sleep well.

(D) Where people spent their resting hours.

(　　) 3. How is the information about the history of bed organized in the passage?

評估詮釋 (A) In order of quality.　　(B) In order of space.

(C) In order of importance.　　(D) In order of time.

(　　) 4. Which of the following can be inferred from this passage?

推論整合 (A) Where people sleep has a lot to do with how well they rest.

(B) As time goes by, the quality of sleep has become better and better.

(C) People have spent more time in bed since the Renaissance.

(D) Ancient people slept better because they rested after sunset.

Unit 2

Study in the US International

Let's Go

美國是世界上最熱門的留學地點之一，本單元提出幾項成為美國留學生所需要經歷的步驟，讓有意去美國留學的讀者，能對申請流程有初步認識。本單元 G.O. 圖搭配 **Sequence Chart (循序圖)** 學習，以下為 **Sequence Chart** 的說明以及示意圖。

說明

1. 循序圖是由有明確開端與結尾的連續事件所構成，多用來解釋事件過程中的步驟或程序。
2. 循序圖與時間線的差別在於：時間線多用於歷史事件，而循序圖則多用於一般事件中，各項過程的階段或步驟。
3. 循序圖的種類包括事件流程圖、問題與解決法圖、因果圖三種。

示意圖

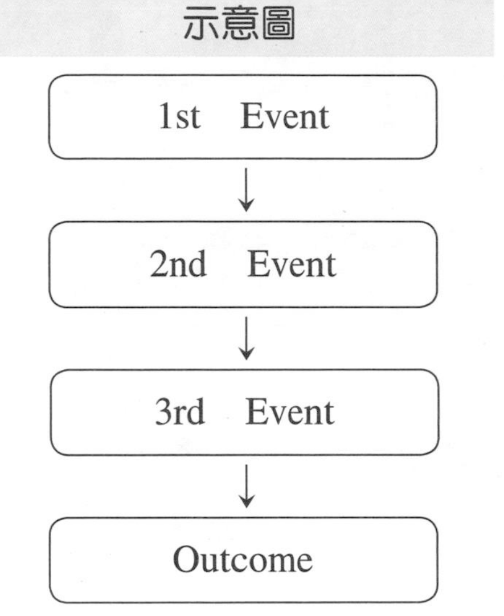

as an Student

❶ The US is one of the most popular places to study in around the world, and for good reason. The US has, along with many of the world's top **academic institutions**, over 4000 first-rate universities. Hence, it may come as no surprise that many groundbreaking advances in science, technology, business, and the arts were first developed in American universities. Once you decide that studying in the US is right for you, there is a 5-step process you need to go through to be ready and eligible.

❷ The first step to become an international student in the US is to **research** your options. The colleges you are interested in should offer the courses and programs you wish to take, be in a desirable location, and be Student and Exchange Visitor Program (SEVP)-certified.

❸ The next step is to **secure finance**. The US government does not provide **loans**, 15 **grants** or scholarships for international students, but there are other ways to **acquire** funds if you or your family are unable to afford the cost. It is possible to receive grants from your local education **authorities**, US-based 20 academic institutions, private **foundations** and businesses, and US government exchange programs.

Words for Production

1. academic *adj.* 學術的
2. institution *n.* [C] 機構
3. research *vt.* 調查，探索
4. secure *vt.* 設法得到
5. finance *n.* [U] 資金
6. loan *n.* [C] 貸款 (需償還)
7. grant *n.* [C] (政府或機構的) 撥款，助學金 (不需償還)
8. acquire *vt.* 獲得
9. authority *n.* [C] 當局
10. foundation *n.* [C] 基金會

Idioms and Phrases

1. along with . . . 除此之外，還有…

Words for Recognition

1. groundbreaking *adj.* 創新的，開創性的
2. eligible *adj.* 有資格的，具備條件的
3. option *n.* [C] 選修課
4. Student and Exchange Visitor Program (SEVP) *n.* 國際學生和交流訪客計劃
5. certified *adj.* 有合格證書的

❹ After you get your funding, you can apply for your desired universities. Any credentials required for entrance will be assessed directly by the institutions you wish to attend. **Furthermore**, you may need to take a standardized test as well as TOEFL, an English proficiency exam.

❺ Once you are accepted by a SEVP certified university, you must apply for a student visa. For this, you will need to fill out an online **application** and schedule an interview at your local US embassy.

6 Finally, you have to ready yourself for life in the US. Make sure you understand the laws, **allowances**, and restrictions of your 35 visa, **including** immigration, employment, and taxes. Find out how to **obtain** a driver's license and perhaps look into courses for learning English as a second language. Learn about the holidays and read up on some 40 useful information about the country. Good luck!

11. furthermore *adv.* 此外，而且
12. application *n.* [C] 申請書
13. allowance *n.* [C] 津貼，補助
14. including *prep.* 包括…
15. obtain *vt.* 獲得

Idioms and Phrases

2. fill out 填寫 (表格等)
3. read up on something (為了得到有關資訊) 廣泛閱讀

Words for Recognition

6. credentials *n. pl.* 資格，資歷
7. assess *vt.* 評估，核定
8. standardized *adj.* 標準化的
9. proficiency *n.* [U] 精熟程度
10. visa *n.* [C] 簽證
11. embassy *n.* [C] 大使館
12. immigration *n.* [U] 移民入境

Graphic Organizer

Pay attention to the clue words (first, next, after, finally, etc.) for sequence in the passage and complete the following sentences in the **Sequence Chart** with the possible answers. Each blank may contain more than one answer. Capitalize the letter when it is needed. The first one has been done for you.

once	~~to start with~~	lastly	~~first of all~~
finally	furthermore	the next stage	besides
second	in addition	~~to begin with~~	after
~~first~~	last but not least	also	next

1 How to study in the US as an international student? [1] First/To begin with/ First of all/To start with , you have to research your options.

2 [2] ________, it is important for you to secure finance because the US government doesn't provide finance for international students.

3 [3] ________ you get your funding, you can apply for your desired universities. [4] ________, you may need to take a standardized English proficiency exam.

4 [5] ________ you're accepted by a SEVP certified university, [6] ________ is to apply for a student visa.

5 [7] ________, you need to ready yourself for life in the US. Good luck!

Reading Comprehension

According to the passage and the following instructions, answer the questions below.

( ) 1. Which of the following is not required when you apply for US universities?

(A)

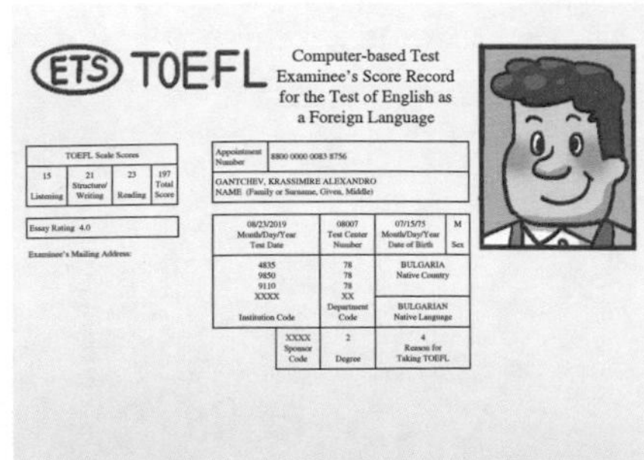

(B)

(C)

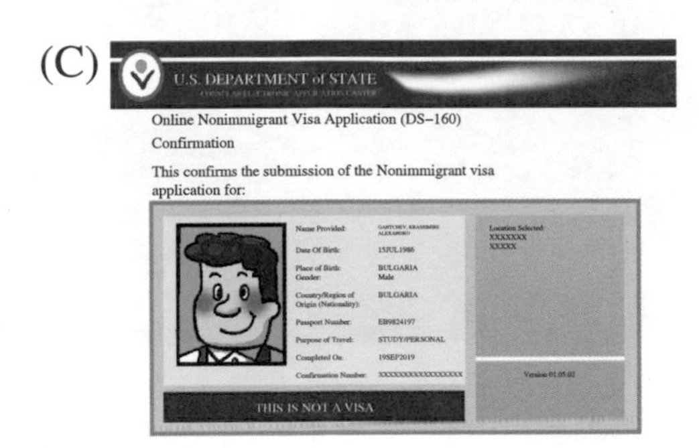

(D)

( ) 2. What is the purpose of this passage?

推論整合 (A) To encourage readers to study in the US.

(B) To help readers gain admission to US universities.

(C) To make clear the process of applying for US universities.

(D) To tell readers how difficult it is to apply for US universities.

( ) 3. According to the passage, which of the following statements is true?

擷取訊息 (A) US universities have made great contributions to academic studies.

(B) US universities are popular because they can be applied online.

(C) The US government provides financial aids for foreign students.

(D) Learning US laws is the last thing that international students should do.

( ) 4. Which of the following may be the reason why a student is unlikely to study in

推論整合 a US university?

(A) The student does not obtain a scholarship.

(B) The student does not have a high TOEFL score.

(C) The student cannot speak American English well.

(D) The student does not have a US student visa.

Let's Go

你有聽過「網路模因」嗎？在這個網路發達的世代，我們有很多機會接收到這類如野火般傳播的訊息。本單元 G.O. 圖搭配 **KWHL Chart (KWHL 表)** 學習，以下為 **KWHL Chart** 的說明以及示意圖。

說明

1. KWHL 表從 KWL 表延伸而來，其中 K 代表「我知道什麼」(What I **K**now)，閱讀前，先確認對主題了解多少；W 代表「我想知道什麼」(What I **W**ant to Know)，想從閱讀中知道些什麼；H 代表「我要如何學習想學的東西」(**H**ow I will learn what I want to learn)；L 代表「我學到了什麼」(What I **L**earned)，閱讀後學到 W 欄位中問題的答案。
2. KWL 表可用於各種領域的課程，填表時必須經過連結、預測、產生問題、澄清、摘要、評鑑等過程，有助於提升閱讀能力。

示意圖

Topic:______			
K	W	H	L

The Viral Nature of **Memes**

❶ Everyone at some point has **encountered** memes. They are humorous words, images, catchphrases, or gifs that spread like wildfire on social media. The term "meme" was first coined by Richard Dawkins, an evolutionary biologist, in his 1976 book, *The Selfish Gene*. He described memes as a form of cultural propagation, ideas that rapidly spread from mind to mind. These ideas can be obvious or complex, and many of them copy the style of human **behavior** in an exaggerated way.

❷ A good example of a meme is an image of Gene Wilder, as Willy Wonka in *Willy Wonka & the Chocolate Factory* with a mocking expression, pretending to be interested in something. This

image along with the sarcastic phrase "tell me more" is often used to make fun of a person's knowledge of something. Memes using the same images and similar phrasing are often 15 customized to express the same idea, but tailored to a specific subject.

3 What makes them so popular and why do they spread so quickly? Memes become memes because they are easy to **distinguish** 20 and understand. They communicate ideas that may require **paragraphs** or even **essays**

Words for Production

1. encounter *vt.* 遇到
2. behavior *n.* [U] 行為，舉止
3. distinguish *vi.* 區分，辨別
4. paragraph *n.* [C] 段落
5. essay *n.* [C] 文章

Idioms and Phrases

1. make fun of 嘲弄

Words for Recognition

1. meme *n.* [C] 模因，模仿傳遞行為 (在網路上迅速傳播的概念、圖像、影像等)
2. catchphrase *n.* [C] 時下流行的話語
3. gif *n.* [C] 一種點陣圖的圖形檔案格式
4. evolutionary *adj.* 進化的
5. biologist *n.* [C] 生物學家
6. propagation *n.* [U] 傳播，宣傳
7. mocking *adj.* 嘲弄的
8. sarcastic *adj.* 嘲諷的
9. customize *vt.* 訂製，客製

to clearly and effectively articulate. Furthermore, **the Internet**, which has enabled instant **communication**, allows memes to reach millions of people in a short space of time. The idea a meme **conveys** can be very simple or deep and meaningful, but regardless of the idea expressed, whether it goes **viral** depends on its **execution**, such as how humorous, **relevant**, striking, absurd, or clear it is.

❹ It doesn't matter how insightful or clever a meme is. **Eventually**, it becomes old and dies. The lifespan of a meme can vary, and its longevity depends on a number of factors. Many memes are the Internet **versions** of fads. Some fall out of fashion quickly, while

others continue to be relevant and are used for years.

❺ At first glance, memes may seem like a less **sophisticated** way to communicate ideas than the written words. On the contrary, just as a picture tells a thousand words, a meme does the same, but also contains a thesis and can spread almost instantly across the globe.

Words for Production

6. the Internet *n. sing.* 網際網路
7. communication *n.* [U] 溝通，交流
8. convey *vt.* 表達，傳達
9. execution *n.* [U] 執行
10. relevant *adj.* 緊密相關的
11. eventually *adv.* 最終
12. version *n.* [C] 版本
13. sophisticated *adj.* 複雜的

Idioms and Phrases

2. regardless of 不管，不論
3. on the contrary 正好相反的是

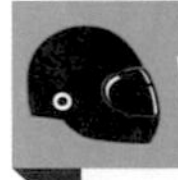

Words for Recognition

10. articulate *vt.* 明確表達，清楚說明
11. absurd *adj.* 荒謬的
12. insightful *adj.* 具洞察力的
13. lifespan *n.* [C] 壽命，有效期
14. longevity *n.* [U] 長壽
15. fad *n.* [C] 短暫的狂熱，一時的風尚
16. thesis *n.* [C] 論點

Graphic Organizer

Look at the **KWHL Chart** and fill in the following blanks with the correct items (A–H) in the box below. The first one has been done for you.

(A) How	~~(B) know~~	(C) what	(D) definition
(E) want	(F) search	(G) learned	(H) mean

Topic: The Viral Nature of Memes			
K	**W**	**H**	**L**
What I [1] (B) about memes?	What I [3] ______ to know about memes?	[5] ______ can I find out more about memes?	What I have [7] ______ about memes?
◆ Though I don't know what memes [2] ______, I guess they are something that will spread quickly.	◆ I want to know [4] ______ a meme is? ◆ I want to find out some examples of memes. ◆ I want to know why and how memes go viral?	◆ I can [6] ______ the Internet to learn more about memes.	◆ I learned the examples of memes. ◆ I learned the [8] ______ and origin of memes. ◆ I learned what makes a successful meme.

Reading Comprehension

According to the passage and the following instructions, answer the questions below.

(　　) 1. What does the word "**viral**" in the third paragraph most likely mean?

評估詮釋 (A) (B) (C) (D)

(　　) 2. According to the passage, which of the following statements about the Willy

推論整合 Wonka meme is true?

(A) Willy Wonka is sincere about what he says.

(B) The words on the image can be changed to fit different situations.

(C) If readers want to know more about something, they can use the meme.

(D) The purpose of the meme is to laugh at a person's facial expression.

(　　) 3. Which of the following is **NOT** the characteristics of memes?

擷取訊息 (A) Exaggerating what people do.

(B) Circulating quickly.

(C) Changing people's behavior.

(D) Involving images and written words.

(　　) 4. Which of the following is **NOT** mentioned in the passage?

推論整合 (A) The expectation of life of a meme.

(B) The example of a meme.

(C) The origin of the word meme.

(D) The pros and cons of a meme.

Let's Go

你可曾看過彷彿卡通人物一般，擁有巨型鳥喙及鮮豔羽毛的巨嘴鳥？本單元介紹巨嘴鳥的外貌、棲地、行為、飲食以及保育，搭配 **Star Diagram (星形圖)** 學習，以下為 **Star Diagram** 的說明以及示意圖。

說明	示意圖
1. 星形圖為圈圈與圈圈的連結，中心部分為單一主題，外側則為多項由該主題延伸的相關概念、事實等內容。 2. 星形圖可用於寫作前的腦力激盪，也可用來回想閱讀完的內容、分類或總結，以作為複習及加深記憶的輔助。	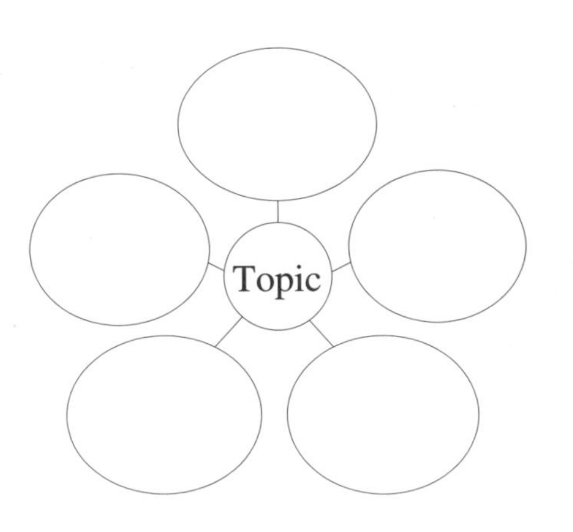

Toucans: The Big-Mouthed Bird

❶ Known for their comically large bills, toucans are one of the most popular bird **species** in the world. The largest and most iconic toucan species, the toco toucan, can grow up to 63 centimeters in length and weigh 620 grams. The color of toucans' feathers varies between subspecies, but it is generally black with touches of white, red, purple, and yellow. The toco toucan, for example, has a black body which strikingly **contrasts** with its white throat and large, vibrant yellow-orange beak.

❷ The toucans' **remarkable** bills are large, in both length and width. Some can even be longer than half the length of their bodies, but they are actually much lighter than they look. The exterior of the

toucan's bill is made of the **protein** keratin. The inside structure of the bill is **composed** of bony fibers which contain a **substantial** number of air pockets. The edges of their 15 beaks are notched, and toucans use these to help them peel and eat large fruits. The toucan's bill also serves to efficiently **regulate** body temperature, which is important in the sweltering heat of the tropical rainforest. 20

❸ Toucans live in the tropical and subtropical regions of South America, from southern Mexico to northern Argentina. They **mostly** live in the forests of large old trees that have holes large enough for them to produce 25 offspring. Toucans are poor travelers and do not migrate. Generally, they hop between trees instead of flying.

Words for Production

1. species *n.* [C] (*pl.* ~) 物種
2. contrast *vi.* 形成對比
3. remarkable *adj.* 引人注目的
4. protein *n.* [U] 蛋白質
5. compose *vt.* 組成，構成
6. substantial *adj.* 大量的
7. regulate *vt.* 控制、調節 (溫度)
8. mostly *adv.* 主要地

Words for Recognition

1. bill *n.* [C] 鳥嘴，喙
2. iconic *adj.* 出名的，代表性的
3. strikingly *adv.* 顯著地
4. vibrant *adj.* 鮮豔的
5. exterior *adj.* 外部的
6. keratin *n.* [U] (羽、髮、角、蹄等的) 角蛋白
7. fiber *n.* [C] 纖維
8. notched *adj.* V 形切口的
9. sweltering *adj.* 酷熱難耐的
10. offspring *n.* [C] (*pl.* ~) 子女，後代
11. migrate *vi.* 遷徙

❹ In terms of their behaviors, toucans are highly sociable, living in groups of up to twenty birds most of their lives. The rest of the time, they pair off to **breed** during the mating season, then return to their groups with their offspring. Toucans primarily eat fruit, but they will eat insects, small lizards, and small birds if the opportunity **arises**. It takes around 35 minutes to digest a meal of fruit, and toucans will not eat again until digestion is complete. They spend this time socializing, such as playing, chasing each other, and calling.

5 Due to their **distinctive** appearance, toucans are one of the more well-known bird species. Traditionally, they were hunted for food, kept as pets, and their feathers (40) and bills were used for **decoration**. In some regions, any one who finds a toucan's nest is **granted** ownership of it and can sell the birds in the nest. Although toucans are not listed as endangered species, the **estimated** (45) populations are **declining**. Unfortunately, many tourists like to buy gifts made of toucan feathers, bills, and so on. Therefore, if you have the chance to pay them a visit, make sure the only things you take home with you (50) are photos of these beautiful birds.

Words for Production

9. breed *vi.* 交配繁殖
10. arise *vi.* 出現，發生
11. distinctive *adj.* 獨特的
12. decoration *n.* [U] 裝飾
13. grant *vt.* 准允
14. estimated *adj.* 估計的
15. decline *vi.* 減少，下降

Idioms and Phrases

1. in terms of
在…方面，從…方面來說
2. pair off 出雙入對，配對
3. pay . . . a visit 拜訪…

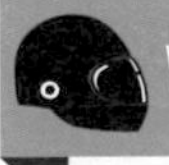

Words for Recognition

12. sociable *adj.* 善於社交的
13. lizard *n.* [C] 蜥蜴
14. endangered species *n.* [C]
瀕危物種

Graphic Organizer

Fill in the missing words to complete the **Star Diagram**. The first one has been done for you.

Appearance

- 63 centimeters in 1 length
- 620 grams in weight
- a black body and a white throat
- a large yellow-orange 2 ______

Habitat

- 3 ______ and subtropical regions of South America
- large holes in the 4 ______ of old trees

Behavior

- very 5 ______
- 6 ______ during the mating season
- playing, chasing each other, and calling

Diet

- mainly 7 ______
- few insects, small lizards and small birds
- 35 minutes to 8 ______ the fruit

Conservation

- be 9 ______ for food
- be kept as pets
- the feathers and bills were used for 10 ______

Reading Comprehension

According to the passage and the following instructions, answer the questions below.

(　　) 1. Which of the following pictures is most likely to be a place where toucans

擷取訊息 live?

(A)

(B)

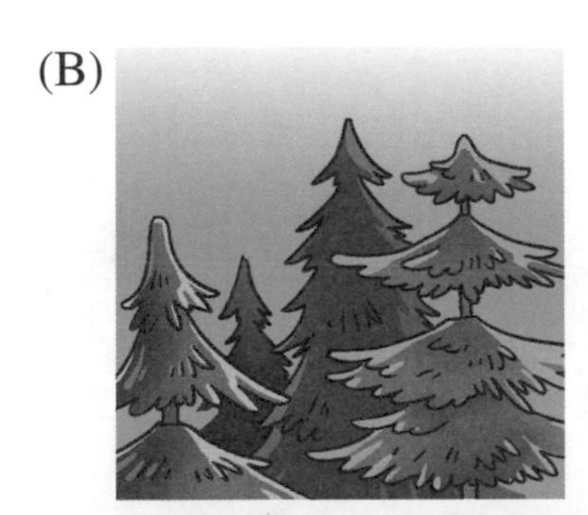

(C)

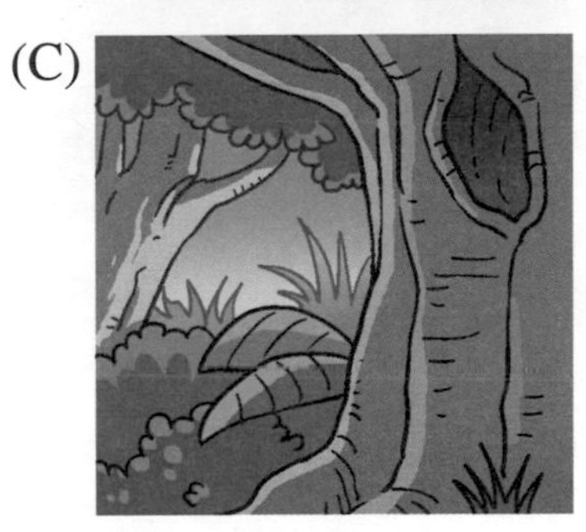

(D)

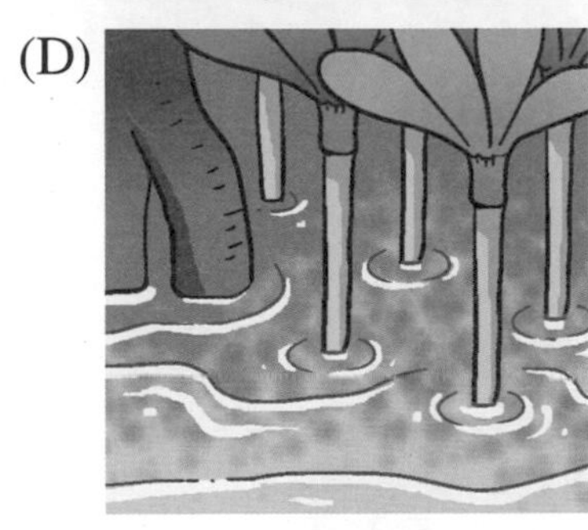

(　　) 2. What causes the number of toucans to decrease?

推論整合 (A) Their sociable behavior. (B) Their unique appearance.

(C) Their overweight black bills. (D) Their special hunting habits.

(　　) 3. Which of the following is the writer's opinion?

評估詮釋 (A) Toucans' bills are made of protein keratin and bony fibers.

(B) Toucans' bills can help regulate their body temperature.

(C) Toucans live in groups in tree holes in South America.

(D) People should avoid purchasing toucans' feathers and bills.

(　　) 4. What can we learn from the passage?

擷取訊息 (A) There are hollow parts in toucans' bills.

(B) Toucans' large bills make them look clumsy.

(C) It takes around one and a half hour for toucans to digest insects.

(D) As there are fewer toucans nowadays, it is illegal to hunt and sell them.

Let's Go

希臘最大、最南端的島嶼——克里特島，以其多樣化的美景聞名於世，其豐富的歷史文化和美味的食物，也讓它成為地中海地區非常著名的度假勝地。本單元 G.O. 圖搭配 **Spider Diagram (蜘蛛圖)** 學習，以下為 **Spider Diagram** 的說明以及示意圖。

說明	示意圖
1. 蜘蛛圖以圖片或文字為中心，而由中心放射延伸出來的數隻「腳」，為中心概念的數個面向。 2. 每個面向為中心概念的次概念，每隻「腳」上，須再添加幾個次概念下的次次概念。 3. 蜘蛛圖以視覺的方式將概念有邏輯地排列，主要用於寫作前的計畫、腦力激盪，也可用來將資料分門別類。	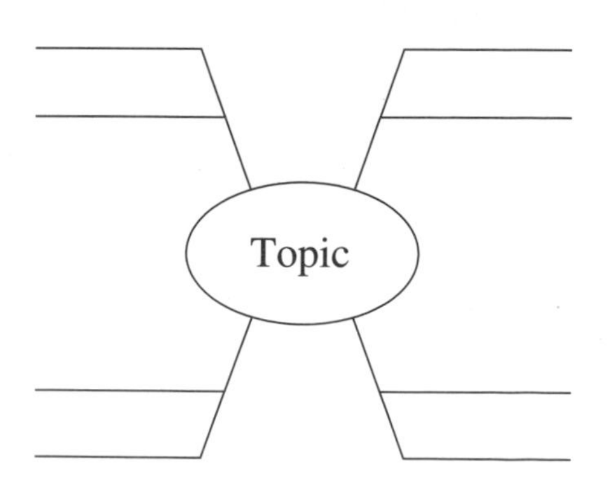

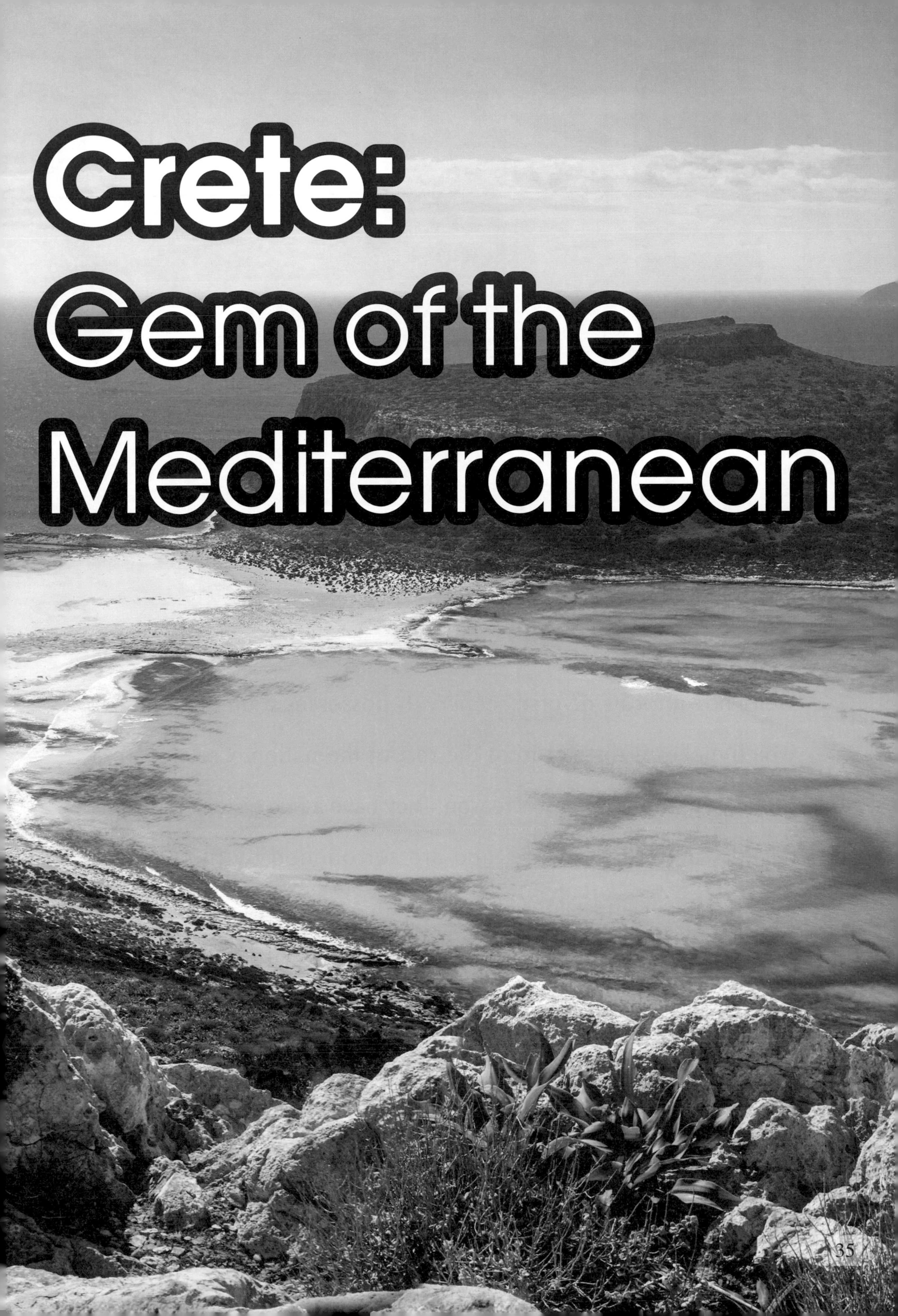

Crete: Gem of the Mediterranean

❶ Crete, the largest and most southerly Greek island, is well-known for its **diverse** scenery. It **possesses** a **unique** culture, which makes it **distinct** from the rest of the nation. Cretans are a proud people and for good reason. They have a rich history, delicious cuisine, a **vibrant** culture, and are surrounded by picturesque Mediterranean **landscapes**.

❷ Without a doubt, the first thing that attracts tourists to holiday in Crete is its beautiful and diverse scenery. With white sandy beaches in the north, **spectacular** coastlines in the south, and **extensive** canyons, deep gorges, snowcapped mountains, and more in between, Crete really does have it all.

❸ The beauty of the island is **enhanced** by the vibrant culture of its **inhabitants**. It is the people of Crete that bring the island to life. Whether it is musicians improvising with traditional instruments, such as the Lyra, or everyday people meeting up at coffee houses for a chat, the people of the island seem to live truly wholesome lives. Cretans are a down-to-earth people, who live in close **communities**.

Words for Production

1. diverse *adj.* 多樣的
2. possess *vt.* 擁有
3. unique *adj.* 獨特的
4. distinct *adj.* 與…截然不同的
5. landscape *n.* [C] 風景
6. spectacular *adj.* 壯麗的
7. extensive *adj.* 廣闊的
8. enhance *vt.* 提升，增強
9. inhabitant *n.* [C] 居民
10. community *n.* [C] 群體

Idioms and Phrases

1. without a doubt 毫無疑問地
2. bring . . . to life 使…更有趣，使…更生動

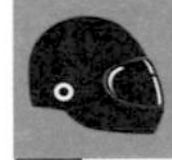

Words for Recognition

1. cuisine *n.* [U] 菜餚
2. picturesque *adj.* 優美的
3. Mediterranean *adj.* 地中海的
4. gorge *n.* [C] 峽谷
5. improvise *vi.* 即興表演
6. Lyra *n.* [C] 里拉琴 (克里特島上的傳統樂器)
7. wholesome *adj* 有益的 (生理和心理層面皆是)
8. down-to-earth *adj.* 務實的

❹ With its rich traditional culture, it is not surprising that Crete also has amazing cuisine. In Crete, village restaurants or taverns produce their own food, including cheeses, meats, olive oil, and wine. They also catch their own seafood. Wherever you go on the island, you will find fresh, authentic, and locally produced foods made with care and passion.

❺ Crete has a rich history dating back to around 2000 B.C. The island was home to the first European civilization, the Minoans. The palace of Knossos was the most **magnificent** building during the Minoan civilization. Since then, Crete's **architecture** has been touched by history in many ways, as can be seen in its Byzantine chapels and churches, 35 Venetian-built cities and fortresses, and Turkish bathhouses and mosques from the time of Ottoman rule.

6 There aren't many places in the world that can claim to have such a rich history, 40 diverse natural scenery, delicious cuisine, and down-to-earth lively people, but Crete is certainly one of them.

Words for Production

11. magnificent *adj.* 壯麗的，宏偉的
12. architecture *n.* [U] 建築設計，建築風格

Idioms and Phrases

3. date back (to . . .) (時間) 追溯 (到⋯)

Words for Recognition

9. tavern *n.* [C] 小酒館
10. authentic *adj.* 正宗的
11. Byzantine *adj.* 拜占庭帝國的
12. chapel *n.* [C] 小教堂
13. Venetian *adj.* 威尼斯式的
14. fortress *n.* [C] 堡壘
15. Turkish *adj.* 土耳其的
16. mosque *n.* [C] 清真寺
17. Ottoman *adj.* 鄂圖曼帝國的

Graphic Organizer

Look at the **Spider Diagram** and fill in the following blanks with the correct items (A–H) in the box below. The first one has been done for you.

(A) traditional	~~(B) scenery~~	(C) history	(D) culture
(E) cuisine	(F) European	(G) spectacular	(H) locally

Crete

1 (B)
- white sandy beaches
- 2 _______ coastlines

3 _______
- 4 _______ instruments
- down-to-earth personality

5 _______
- cheeses, meats, olive oil, wine, and seafood
- authentic 6 _______ produced foods

7 _______
- dating back to around 2000 B.C.
- home to the first 8 _______ civilization

Reading Comprehension

According to the passage and the following instructions, answer the questions below.

(　　) 1. According to the passage, which of the following may be a travel brochure for

擷取訊息 Crete?

(　　) 2. What does the word "**vibrant**" in the first paragraph most likely mean?

評估詮釋 (A) Violent.　(B) Shaking.　(C) Ancient.　(D) Lively.

(　　) 3. According to the passage, which of the following statements is true?

擷取訊息 (A) Crete's rich architecture is influenced by its long and diverse history.

(B) People in Crete are rich because tourism has made them rich.

(C) Crete's picturesque Mediterranean scenery is unique in Greece.

(D) Cretans are busy making their living by running restaurants.

(　　) 4. Where does this passage most likely appear?

推論整合 (A) In a breaking news report.　(B) In a Michellin Guide.

(C) On Trip Advisor.　(D) In a history textbook.

Why Are **Whales** Left Stranded

Let's Go

鯨魚是海洋中的大型哺乳類動物，然而碩大的體型並不能保證牠們的安全，有什麼原因會造成鯨魚擱淺、死亡呢？本單元 G.O. 圖搭配 **Fishbone Diagram (魚骨圖)** 學習，以下為 **Fishbone Diagram** 的說明以及示意圖。

說明

1. 魚骨圖包含魚頭及身體骨頭，常用在因果分析。
2. 魚頭為問題或結果，身體的骨頭則為導致此問題或結果的因素。
3. 依據因素的層級，大骨頭表示主要原因，次要以及更次要的原因，則分別列在中骨頭及小骨頭上。

示意圖

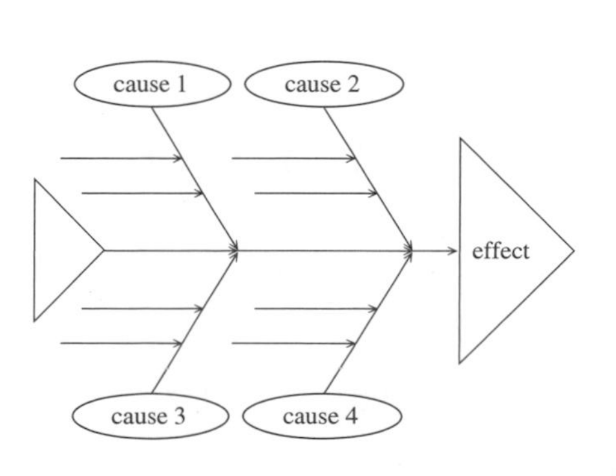

❶ Whales are the great mammals of the sea and are among the largest animals on earth. They roam and migrate thousands of kilometers through the ocean, hunting and socializing with their group or pod. However, their large size does not guarantee their safety. One of the major causes of whale deaths is **stranding**. It may seem hard to believe but whales do strand themselves on beaches once in a while. Cetacean stranding is the

phenomenon in which whales and dolphins become stuck in shallow water or on beaches. **Despite** the fact that it's difficult to know the exact cause of whale stranding, experts have found a range of factors that alone or in **combination** could result in whales becoming stranded.

❷ First, many beached whales are either old or sick. These whales become stranded because they can't keep up with the rest of their group, or they are not strong enough to resist the swells of the ocean pulling them to shore. Whales can be sick or in poor health in a number of ways such as from temporary natural illness, the buildup of toxins and heavy metals, or a lack of food due to overfishing. These factors can cause them to become disoriented, affecting their ability to navigate, or simply making them too weak to avoid being washed up on the shore.

Words for Production

1. strand *vt.* 使滯留、擱淺
2. phenomenon *n.* [C] 現象
3. despite *prep.* 儘管
4. combination *n.* [U] 結合

Idioms and Phrases

1. once in a while 偶爾地
2. result in 導致，結果造成
3. keep up with 跟上，並駕齊驅
4. wash something up 把…沖到陸地上

Words for Recognition

1. mammal *n.* [C] 哺乳動物
2. roam *vi.* 徜徉
3. pod *n.* [C] (海豚或鯨等海洋動物的) 一群
4. cetacean *n.* [C] 鯨類
5. toxin *n.* [C] 毒素
6. disoriented *adj.* 迷失方向的
7. navigate *vi.* 導航，確定方向

30 ❸ Another factor that can lead to whale stranding is injury. Collisions with ships or nets can cause innumerable kinds of injuries, which may contribute to the whales being stranded on a beach. Additionally, loud noises caused by man-made underwater **explosions** or sea quakes can **severely** damage a whale's hearing,
35 affecting its ability to navigate, hunt, and communicate.

❹ Whales may also be left stranded due to simple navigational errors, such as swimming too close to the shore. Shallow waters with a long, gentle slope can interfere with a whale's echolocation, so it may lack **information** about its **surroundings**. 40 Furthermore, coastlines that whales are unfamiliar with and extreme weather conditions are both **potential** factors that may lead to navigational errors.

5 Lastly, stranding can occur owing to 45 social bonding. Many whale species develop strong social bonds with their pod. This can sometimes result in mass stranding. When a single whale is stranded, the rest of the pod follows. This phenomenon most often occurs 50 with pilot whales that have highly complex social structures.

Words for Production

5. explosion *n.* [C] 爆裂 (聲)
6. severely *adv.* 嚴重地
7. information *n.* [U] 資訊
8. surroundings *n. pl.* 環境
9. potential *n.* [U] 可能性

Idioms and Phrases

5. interfere with something 干擾…，妨礙…

Words for Recognition

8. collision *n.* [C] 碰撞，相撞
9. innumerable *adj.* 無數的，數不清的
10. echolocation *n.* [U] 回聲定位
11. bonding *n.* [U] 與…的親密關係聯結

Graphic Organizer

Fill in the missing words to complete the **Fishbone Diagram**. The first one has been done for you.

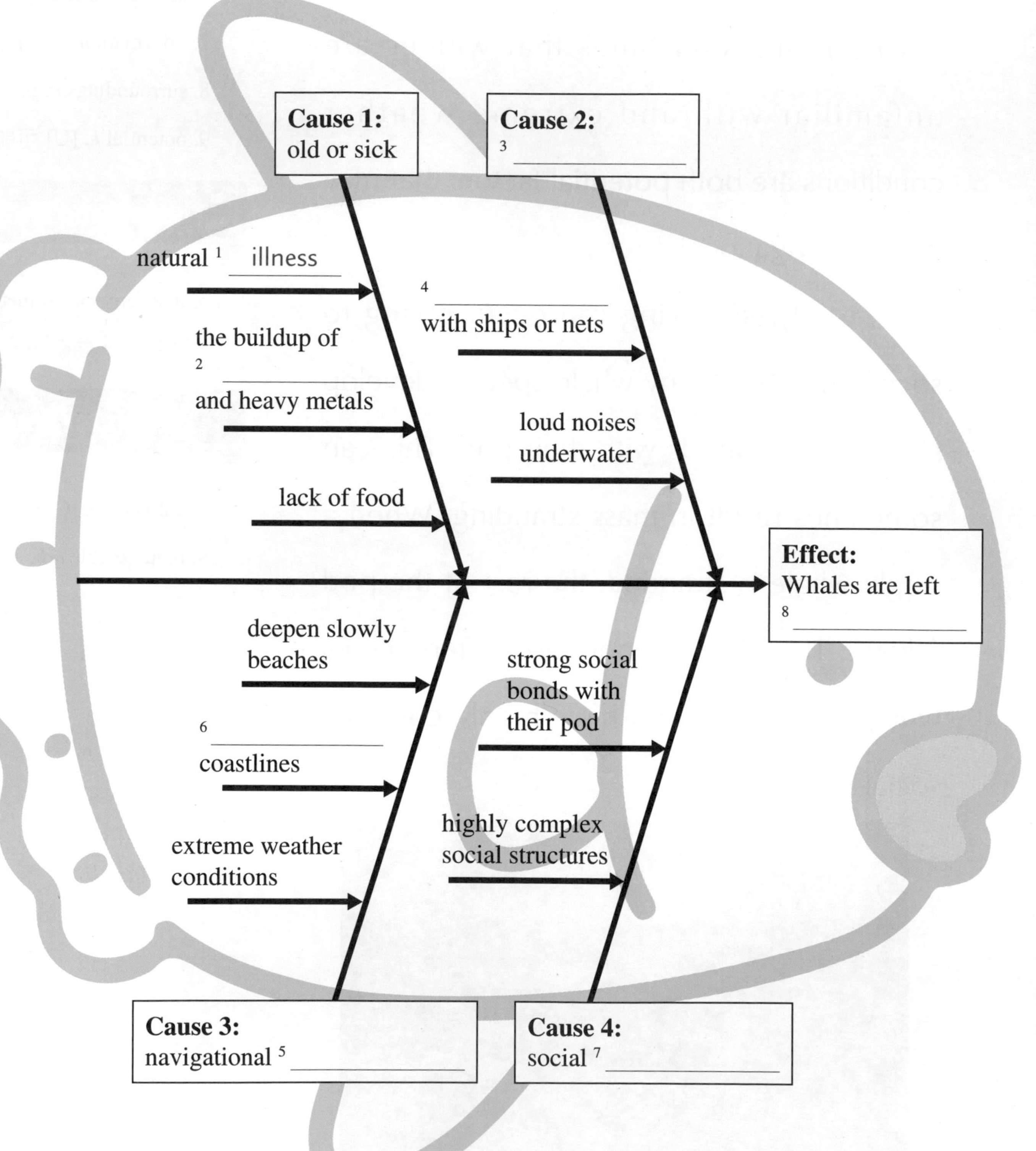

Reading Comprehension

According to the passage and the following instructions, answer the questions below.

(　　) 1. Which picture best describes the phenomenon in the passage?

評估詮釋 (A)

(B)

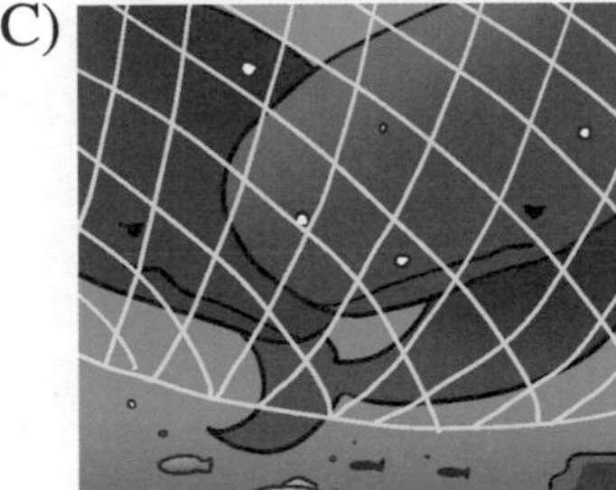

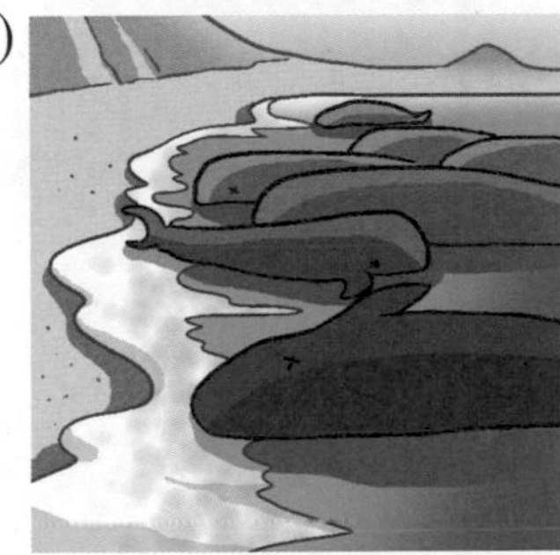

(　　) 2. What is the passage mainly about?

推論整合 (A) The causes of whales being washed ashore.

(B) The reasons for the decreasing number of whales.

(C) The ways that fishermen catch whales.

(D) The places in which whales get stuck.

(　　) 3. Which is the final reason for whales getting stranded on beaches?

擷取訊息 (A) They are in poor health.

(B) They lose their navigational abilities.

(C) They lose their hearing.

(D) They leave their group or pod.

(　　) 4. Which of the following can be inferred from this passage?

推論整合 (A) A lot of whales commit suicide on beaches.

(B) Many whales are killed by sea earthquakes.

(C) Whales migrate with dolphins and other fish.

(D) Sea water is polluted by heavy metals.

Let's Go

小麥製品，如麵包和義大利麵，是許多人的主食，然而小麥這項原料，可能造成幾項健康上的問題。本單元 G.O. 圖搭配 **Tree Diagram (樹狀圖)** 學習，以下為 **Tree Diagram** 的說明以及示意圖。

說明	示意圖
1. 樹狀圖與家庭樹概念相同，第一層樹幹代表主題，第二層樹枝代表相關的事實、因素、影響、特色、結果等，依此再往下列出第三層、第四層等支持細節。 2. 樹狀圖常用於分類與組織資料，使主題和細項之間層次更清楚明瞭。	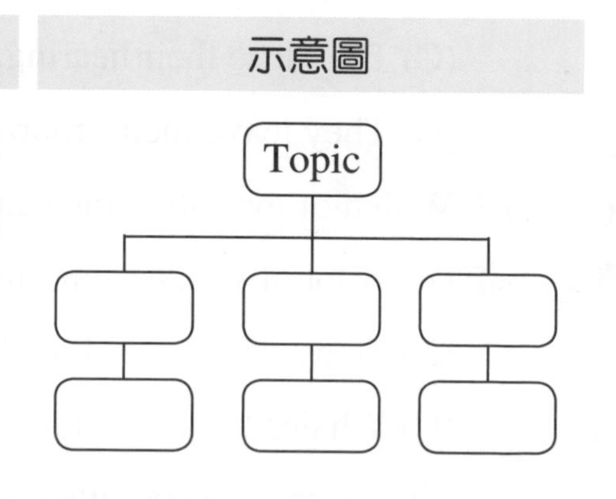

The **Wheat** Problem

❶ Bread and pasta are staple foods for many people, but studies have shown that their main **ingredient**, wheat, is the cause of **numerous** health problems plaguing the modern world. Wheat belongs to the grass family and is cultivated for its seeds as a **relatively** cheap food source. While wheat **production** may give the world's population **access** to an affordable source of energy, its **consumption** comes at a cost.

❷ The fiberless carbohydrates in wheat are so easily **absorbed** by the human body that they cause large spikes in blood sugar. The human body cannot **cope** with too much sugar in the blood so it is **converted** into fat which can lead to obesity. Furthermore, most of this fat is stored around the organs, which is linked to heart disease.

❸ Spikes in blood sugar also require the body to produce an equally large spike of insulin in response. However, **overexposure** 15 to insulin often causes cells to develop insulin **resistance**, leading to type 2 diabetes. What's more, elevated blood sugar leaves behind toxic chemicals that gather in the skin, which ages your skin, making your skin dry and 20 wrinkled.

Words for Production

1. ingredient *n.* [C] 材料
2. numerous *adj.* 眾多的
3. relatively *adv.* 相對地
4. production *n.* [U] 生產
5. access *n.* [U] 使用的機會
6. consumption *n.* [U] 食用量
7. absorb *vt.* 吸收
8. cope *vi.* 處理
9. convert *vt.* 轉化
10. overexposure *n.* [U] 過度暴露於…
11. resistance *n.* [U] 抵抗

Words for Recognition

1. staple *adj.* 主要的
2. plague *vt.* 使受折磨，困擾
3. cultivate *vt.* 栽種，培育
4. fiberless *adj.* 無纖維的
5. carbohydrate *n.* [C] 碳水化合物，醣類
6. spike *n.* [C] 猛增，急升
7. obesity *n.* [U] 肥胖
8. insulin *n.* [U] 胰島素
9. diabetes *n.* [U] 糖尿病
10. elevated *adj.* 偏高的

❹ Wheat is also associated with a number of intolerances, which cause inflammation in the body. The **symptoms** of this inflammation include skin rashes, swelling, and even baldness.

25 ❺ Wheat consumption can have **psychological** effects as well. Research has shown many people have better mood, deeper sleep, and greater **concentration** after cutting wheat from their diets. However, kicking the wheat habit can be a challenge. About 30 percent of people who **eliminated** wheat from their diet experienced 30 withdrawal symptoms such as extreme fatigue, unstable emotions, and brain fog. These symptoms suggest that wheat is addictive. In some cases, wheat can even cause hallucinations. A 72-year-old woman

who had suffered from regular hallucinations had stopped having them after eight days of not eating wheat. 35

❻ Eating wheat is not all bad, though. Studies suggest that foods rich in carbohydrates have an uplifting effect on mood shortly after being eaten. But wheat is not the only food that contains carbohydrates. 40 In conclusion, it seems that the benefits of giving up wheat significantly outweigh the downsides.

Words for Production

12. symptom *n.* [C] 症狀
13. psychological *adj.* 心理的
14. concentration *n.* [U] 專注
15. eliminate *vt.* 消除

Idioms and Phrases

1. be associated with 與…連結

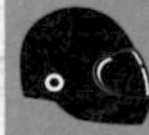

Words for Recognition

11. intolerance *n.* [C] 過敏
12. inflammation *n.* [U] 發炎
13. withdrawal symptoms *n. pl.* 脫癮症狀
14. fatigue *n.* [U] 疲勞
15. hallucination *n.* [C] 幻覺
16. uplifting *adj.* 令人振奮的
17. downside *n.* [C] 缺點

Graphic Organizer

Look at the **Tree Diagram** and fill in the following blanks with the correct items (A–H) in the box below. The first one has been done for you.

(A) swelling	(B) skin rashes	(C) obesity
(D) emotions	~~(E) blood sugar~~	(F) addiction

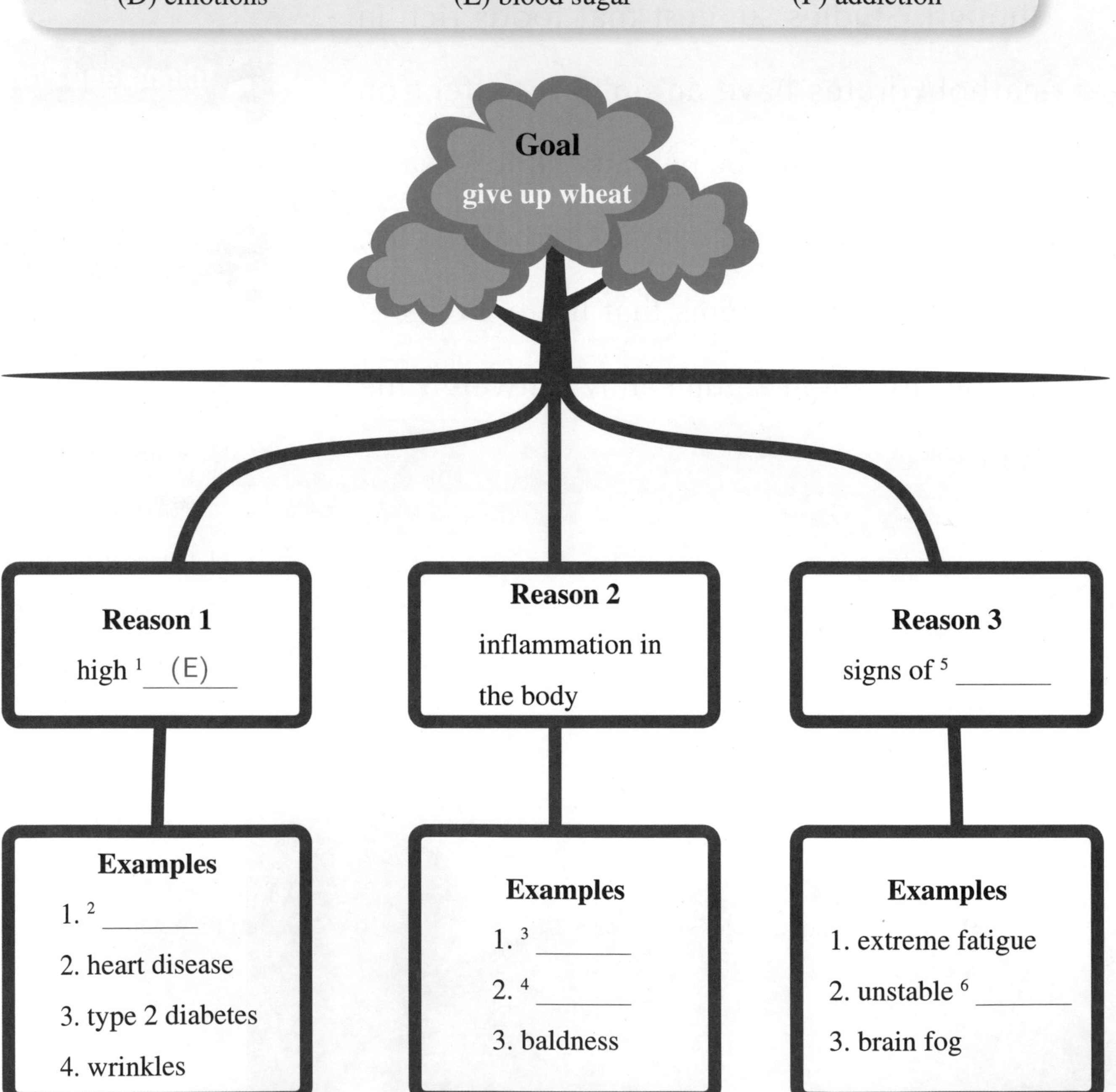

Reading Comprehension

According to the passage and the following instructions, answer the questions below.

(　　) 1. Which of the following graphs shows the correct cause-effect relationship?

擷取訊息

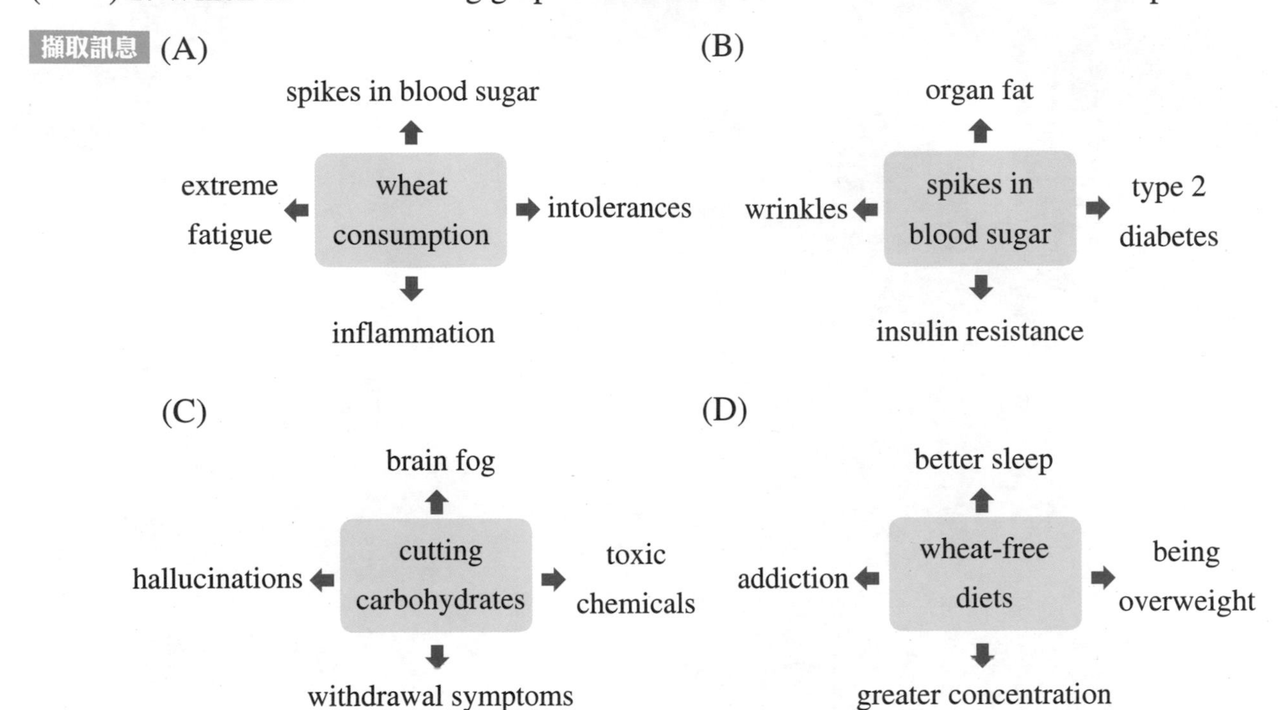

(　　) 2. What is the purpose of this passage?

推論整合 (A) To persuade readers to consume less cheap food.

(B) To teach readers how to control blood sugar.

(C) To inform readers of the cause of heart disease.

(D) To discourage readers from eating wheat.

(　　) 3. Which of the following is **NOT** used to support the author's viewpoint?

評估詮釋 (A) Statistics.　(B) Researches.　(C) News reports.　(D) Examples.

(　　) 4. According to the passage, which of the following statements is true?

擷取訊息 (A) The advantages of eating wheat include its low cost and its positive effect on mood.

(B) Type 2 diabetes causes cells to become resistant to insulin.

(C) Carbohydrates in wheat make people sleepy, unhealthy, and older.

(D) It takes people quite a long time to get used to diets without wheat.

Let's Go

動物實驗一直以來是個頗具爭議的議題，一方面，它對醫療突破有所貢獻；但另一方面，卻要動物受苦作為代價。你是如何看待動物實驗的呢？本單元 G.O. 圖搭配 **T-Chart (T 形圖)** 學習，以下為 **T-Chart** 的說明以及示意圖。

說明	示意圖
1. T 形圖是一個 T 字組成的圖表，常用於分析或比較一個情況或事件的兩面。 2. T 形圖於閱讀或寫作說明文時，可用於分析優點與缺點、問題與解決法、事實與意見、相同與相異之處等。	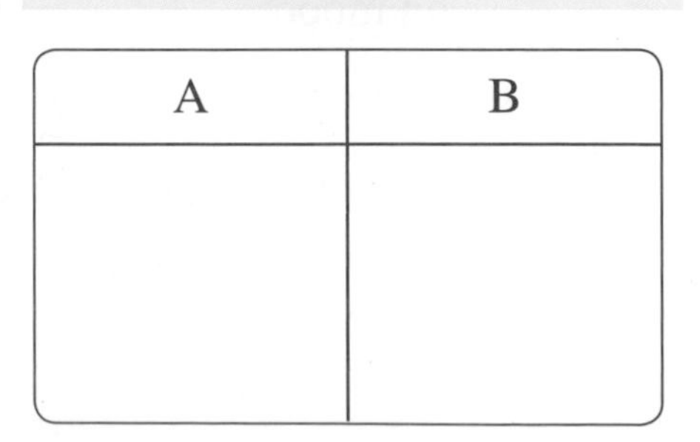

Animal Testing: For and Against

❶ Animal testing has long been a **controversial issue**. On the one hand, it **contributes** to medical breakthroughs that could greatly benefit mankind, but on the other hand, it comes at the expense of animal suffering. Thus, we are faced with a moral **dilemma** when it comes to testing products on animals. However you look at it, someone or something always loses out. The question is whether or not it is worth it.

❷ Genetically, humans share about 90 **percent** of their DNA with mice. Therefore, animal testing on mice provides scientists with a way to conduct tests on living bodies that not only have functioning organs and systems, but also have most of the genes that humans possess. Besides, testing on animals can be much more effective than other methods. The shorter lifespans of animals like mice allow us to study the effects of medications and treatments over a lifetime or even **multiple generations** in a short period of time. In fact, animal testing has been **crucial** in the development of most life-saving cures and treatments. Nearly every breakthrough in the last century has resulted from the use of testing on animals.

❸ In Taiwan, all new promising substances, from medicines to cosmetics, are **regulated** so that they need to be tested on animals to **ensure** they are safe for humans to use. Although it is impossible to find every harmful substance during animal testing, it is still an important method of reducing the risk of harm to humans at present. What's more, animals themselves benefit from animal testing too. Without it, many of the vaccines and treatments for diseases that animals suffer from would never have been made.

Words for Production

1. controversial *adj.* 具爭議性的
2. issue *n.* [C] 議題
3. contribute *vi.* 對…有貢獻
4. dilemma *n.* [C] 進退兩難的困境
5. percent *n. sing.* 百分之…
6. multiple *adj.* 多次的
7. generation *n.* [C] 世代
8. crucial *adj.* 至關重要的
9. regulate *vt.* (用規則條例) 約束，管理
10. ensure *vt.* 保證

Idioms and Phrases

1. on the one hand **. . .** on the other hand **. . .** 一方面…另一方面…
2. at the expense of **. . .** 以…為代價的情況下
3. at present 目前，當下

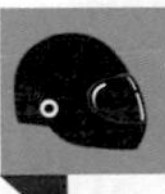

Words for Recognition

1. breakthrough *n.* [C] 重大進展，突破
2. genetically *adv.* 基因上
3. medication *n.* [C] 藥物
4. cosmetics *n. pl.* 化妝品
5. vaccine *n.* [C] 疫苗

④ Despite the advantages of using animals for research, there are **definitely** some downsides. The most obvious is the cruelty of subjecting living creatures to these tests. Animals can suffer just like humans, so why is it acceptable to put them through these experiments?

⑤ Another problem with animal testing is reliability. While some animals are similar to humans, they are still different and may be poor test subjects. Many drugs that pass animal tests end up being unsafe for humans or simply do not work. This wastes the lives of the animals, along with significant amounts of money too. Furthermore, medications that could be safe and effective for humans may never be discovered if they 45 are found to be unsafe for animals.

❻ In conclusion, animal testing should be strictly regulated. Researchers are required to treat animal test subjects as humanely as possible and carefully consider the necessity 50 of animal testing. After all, some important medical breakthroughs could have been made without the use of animals in the first place. Hopefully, **alternative** methods can be found as soon as possible so that relatively 55 few animals will be needed for research purposes in the future.

Words for Production

11. definitely *adv.* 確實地
12. alternative *adj.* 可供替代的

Idioms and Phrases

4. end up 最終成為，最後處於
5. in the first place (用於句尾) 當初，原本

Words for Recognition

6. reliability *n.* [U] 可信度
7. humanely *adv.* 人道地

Pay attention to the pros and cons of animal testing in the passage and fill in the missing words to complete the **T-Chart**. The first one has been done for you.

Introduction

Animal testing has long been a [1] controversial issue.

Pros ✓

1. Animal testing [2] ____________ to medical breakthroughs.
2. Animals share [3] ____________ genes with humans.
3. The shorter lifespans of animals help to study the effects of treatments effectively.
4. Animal testing is [4] ____________ to most life-saving cures and treatments.
5. New substances of cosmetics or medicines must be tested on animals to [5] ____________ their safety.
6. Animal themselves [6] ____________ from animal testing.

Cons ✗

1. Animal testing is [7] ____________ and inhumane.
2. Animal testing makes animals [8] ____________.
3. Animals are [9] ____________ from human beings.
4. Drugs that pass animal tests are not necessarily safe.
5. Animal testing [10] ____________ the lives of the animals.
6. Animal testing costs significant amounts of money.

Conclusion

Animal testing should be strictly [11] ____________. Hopefully, [12] ____________ methods can be found as soon as possible.

Reading Comprehension

According to the passage and the following instructions, answer the questions below.

(　　) 1. Which of the following has nothing to do with animal testing?

擷取訊息 (A)

(B)

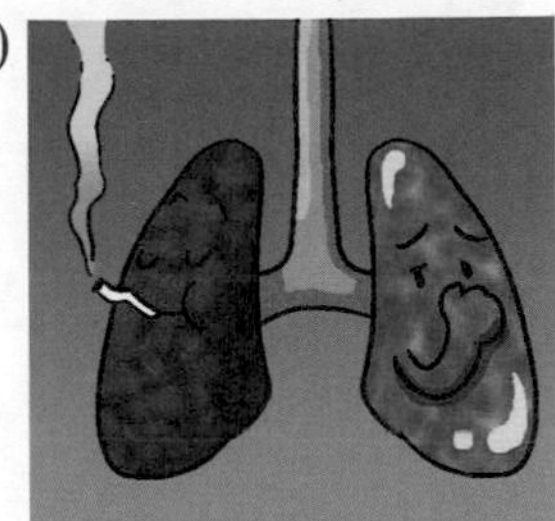

(C)

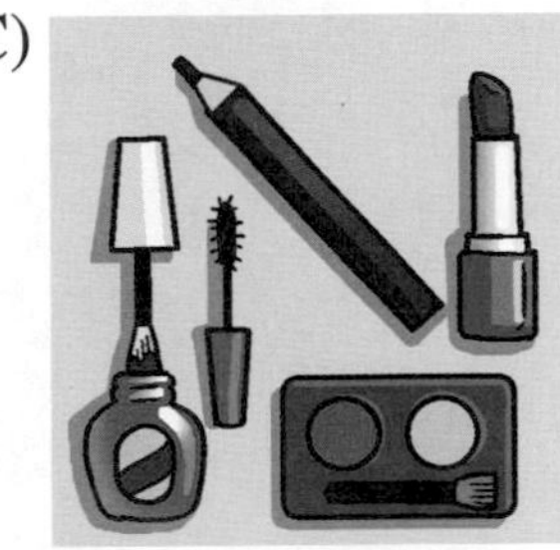

(D)

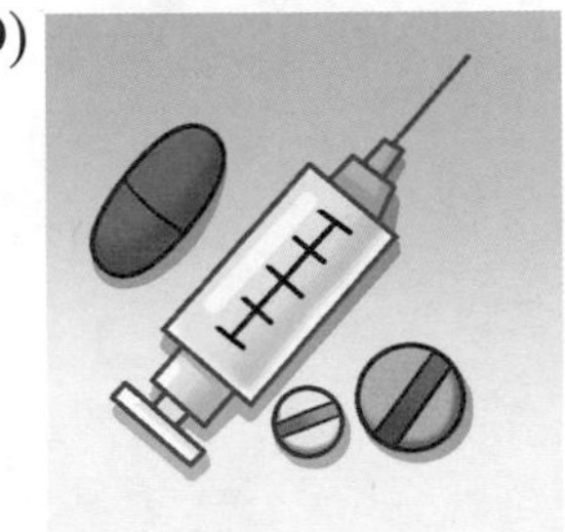

(　　) 2. Which of the following statements is **NOT** included in this passage?

評估詮釋 (A) The reasons for mice being tested. (B) The problems with animal testing.

(C) How animal testing helps animals. (D) How scientists do animal testing.

(　　) 3. Which of the following best describes the author's attitude toward animal testing?

推論整合

(A) Animal testing is so cruel that it should be banned.

(B) Animal testing should be promoted all over the world.

(C) Animal testing should be avoided unless it is necessary.

(D) Animal testing is only for the benefits of humans and animals.

(　　) 4. Which of the following can be inferred from this passage?

推論整合 (A) Without animal testing, scientists could not make any medical breakthroughs.

(B) Those who are opposed to testing on animals care a lot about animal rights.

(C) More and more countries will enforce laws to stop using animals for testing.

(D) Animal testing is a debatable topic now, but the argument will soon be settled.

Unit 9

Let's Go

提到超級病毒，很多在臺灣的人們腦中浮現的會是禽流感和 SARS，這兩者有許多相似之處，卻也有各自不同的地方。本單元G.O.圖搭配 Venn Diagram (文氏圖) 學習，以下為 Venn Diagram 的說明以及示意圖。

說明	示意圖
1. 文氏圖一般由兩個圓圈部分重疊而成，主要用來比較與對比兩個事物相同與相異之處，中間重疊的部分為相同之處，兩旁不重疊的部分為相異之處。 2. 抽象的概念或複雜的關係可透過文氏圖比較與對比將其視覺化，以釐清思考方向。	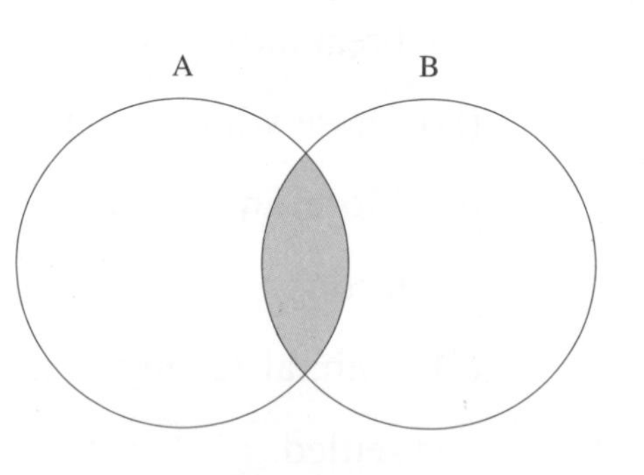

Bird Flu vs. SARS: Similarities and Differences

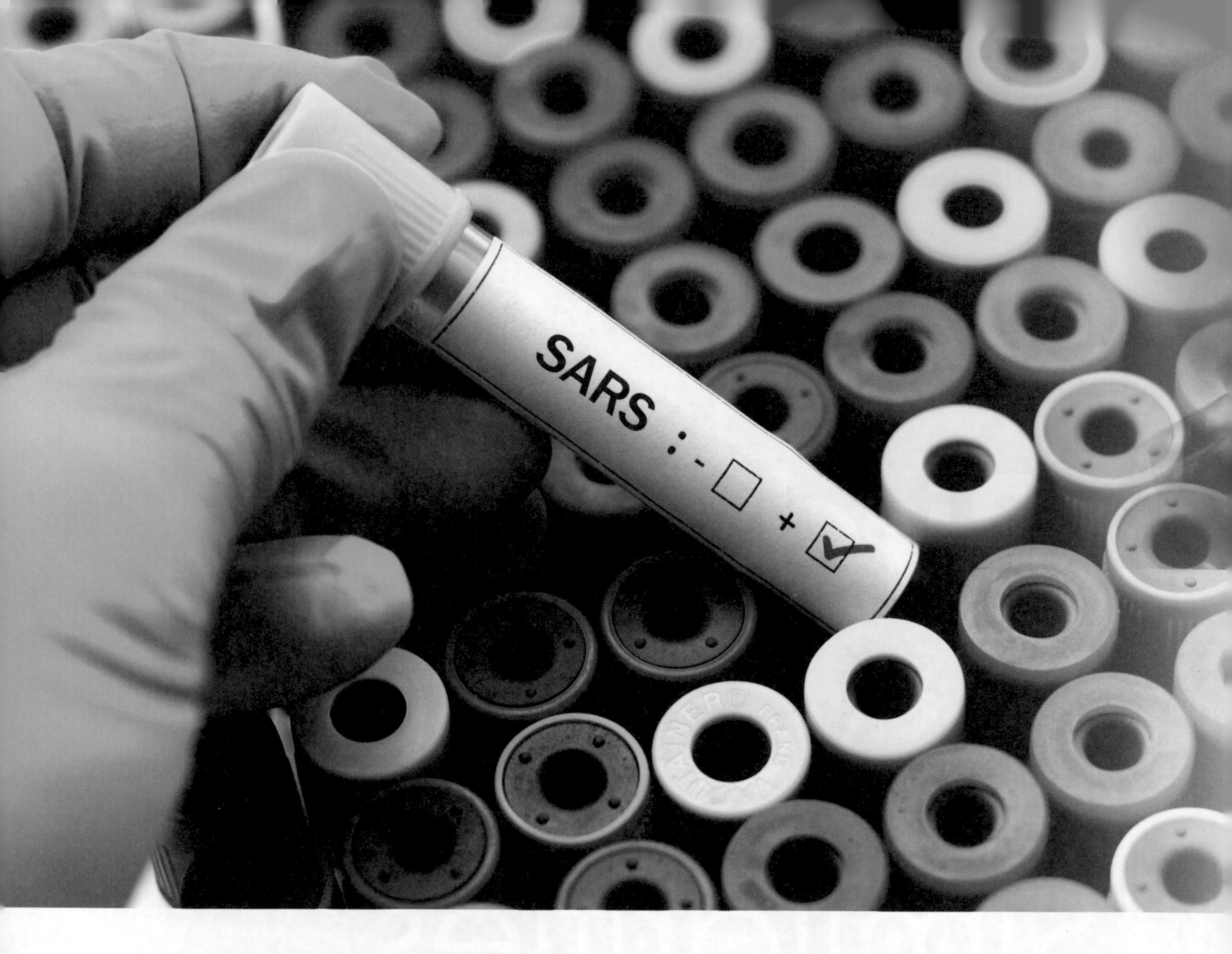

❶ Every year when flu season comes around, there is always a lot of attention given by the media to the **prevention** of **infection**. Sometimes, it isn't just the common cold or flu that is going around, but something more serious. Speaking of super **viruses**, bird flu and SARS may be the two that come to mind for many people in Taiwan.

❷ The bird flu and SARS viruses are similar in various ways. They both enter human bodies through the nose and mouth and lead to respiratory infections. They also cause similar symptoms, such as fever and breathing difficulties. What's more, they may even be **fatal**, unlike the common cold and most other types of flu. Additionally,

both viruses affect only animals until they mutate, which enable them to infect humans. Currently, there is no known cure for either bird flu or SARS.

❸ In spite of the similarities between bird 15 flu and SARS, there are quite a few significant differences. While bird flu, as the name suggests, is a **strain** of flu virus, the SARS virus is more closely related to the common cold. Bird flu cannot, as yet, be **transferred** easily 20

Words for Production

1. prevention *n.* [U] 預防
2. infection *n.* [U][C] 傳染，感染
3. virus *n.* [C] 病毒
4. fatal *adj.* 致命的
5. strain *n.* [C] (疾病的) 類型，品種
6. transfer *vt.* 傳染，轉移 (疾病)

Idioms and Phrases

1. come around (定期發生的事件) 來臨，發生
2. go around 流傳，傳播
3. come to mind 突然記起，想到
4. as yet 直到現在

Words for Recognition

1. bird flu *n.* [U] 禽流感
2. SARS *n.* [U] (= severe acute respiratory syndrome) 嚴重急性呼吸道症候群
3. respiratory *adj.* 呼吸的
4. mutate *vi.* 突變

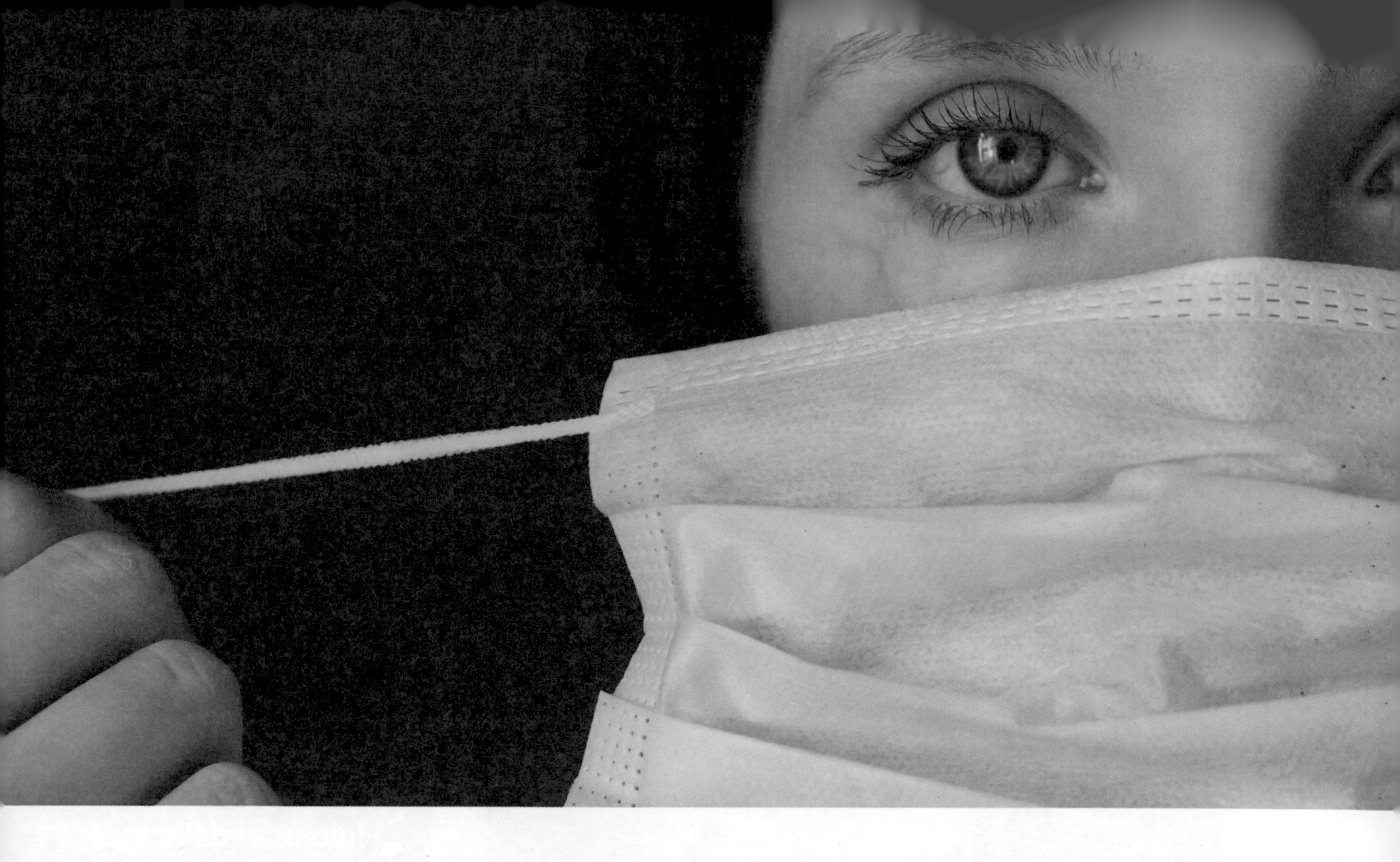

from human to human. SARS, on the other hand, can be **transmitted** rapidly between people. However, experts believe that if bird flu were to mutate and be capable of human to human **transmission**, it would be far more contagious than SARS. Despite being much harder to contract, bird flu is significantly deadlier than SARS. Up to 50 percent of people infected with bird flu die, **whereas** SARS only has a 10 percent mortality rate. Furthermore, the last confirmed case of SARS was in 2003, unlike bird flu, which has been on the rise in recent years.

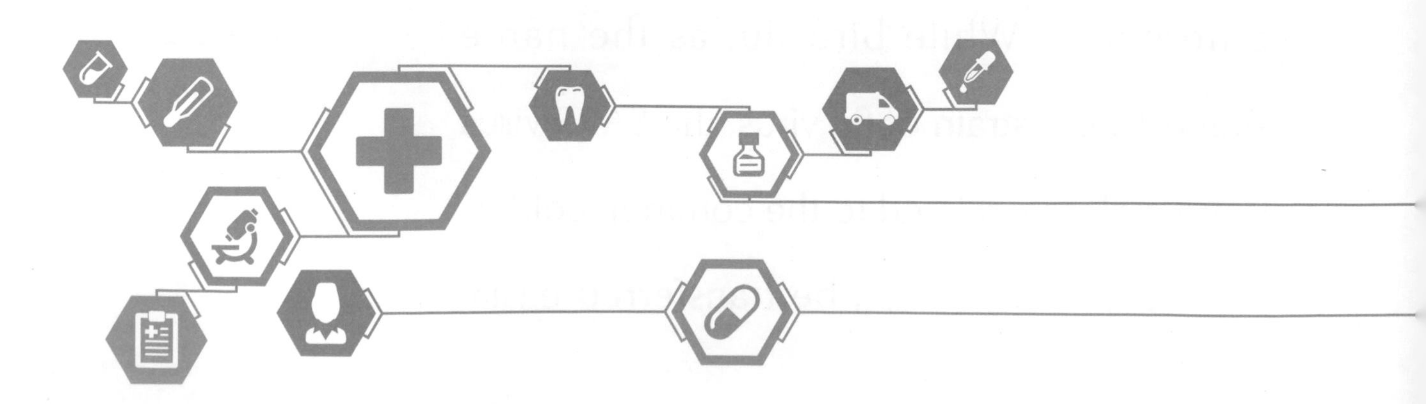

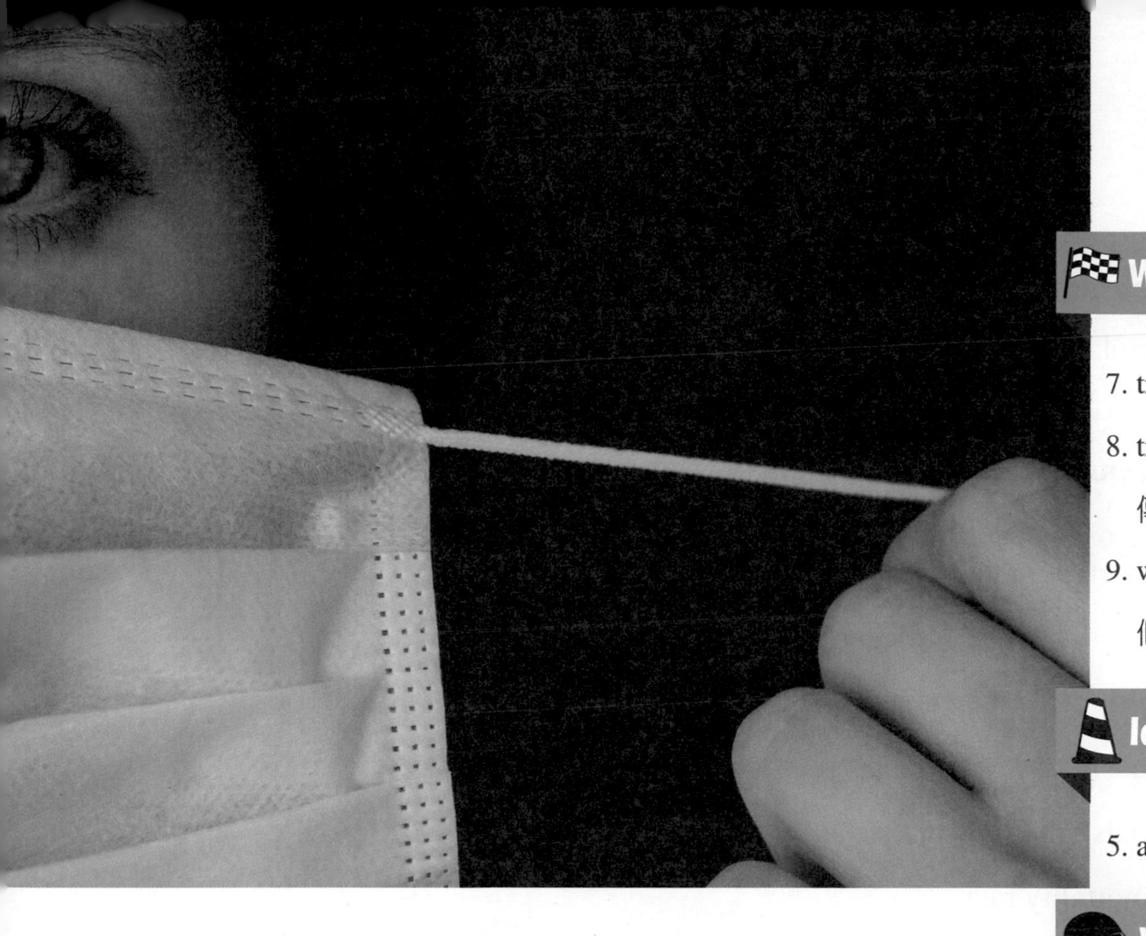

Words for Production

7. transmit *vt.* 傳播，傳染
8. transmission *n.* [U] 傳播，傳染
9. whereas *conj.* (用以比較兩個事實) 然而，但是

Idioms and Phrases

5. all in all 總之

Words for Recognition

5. contagious *adj.* (疾病) 接觸傳染的
6. deadly *adj.* (可能) 致命的
7. mortality *n.* [U] 死亡，死亡數量
8. hygiene *n.* [U] 衛生

4 If you are planning to travel to a region (30) affected by either of these viruses, it is crucial to practice good hygiene. The most important thing you can do to avoid infection is to wash your hands regularly and take care not to touch your face, especially your nose and (35) eyes. All in all, you can never be too careful when it comes to these deadly viruses.

Graphic Organizer

Find out the similarities and differences between bird flu and SARS in the passage. Then, fill in the following blanks with the correct items (A–F) in the box below to complete the **Venn Diagram**. The first one has been done for you.

(A) a lower mortality rate

~~(B) can only be transmitted from an infected bird to a human~~

(C) lead to respiratory infections

(D) can be transmitted between people

(E) only animals until they mutate to be able to infect humans

(F) a higher mortality rate

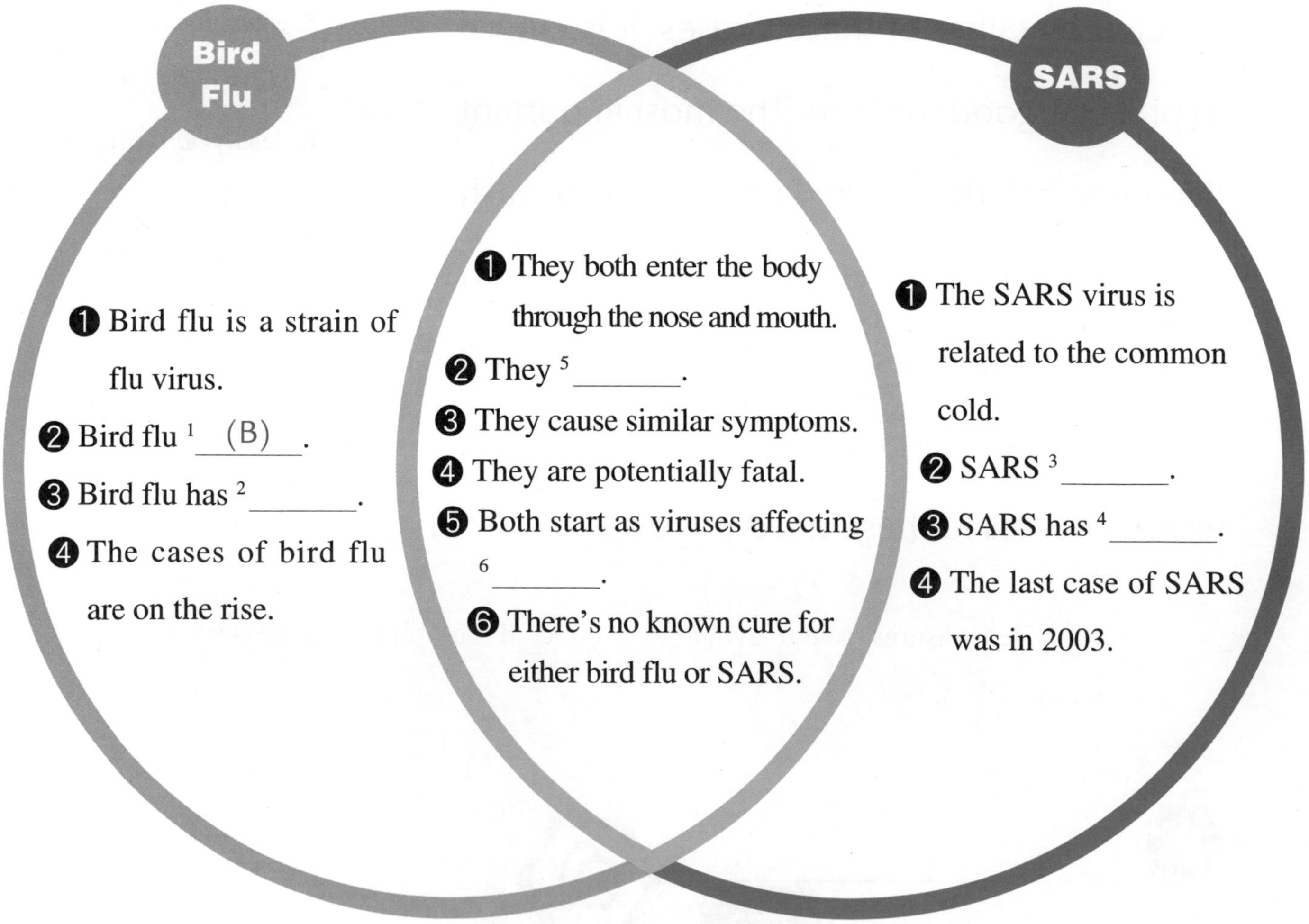

Bird Flu

❶ Bird flu is a strain of flu virus.

❷ Bird flu [1] (B).

❸ Bird flu has [2] _______.

❹ The cases of bird flu are on the rise.

Both

❶ They both enter the body through the nose and mouth.

❷ They [5] _______.

❸ They cause similar symptoms.

❹ They are potentially fatal.

❺ Both start as viruses affecting [6] _______.

❻ There's no known cure for either bird flu or SARS.

SARS

❶ The SARS virus is related to the common cold.

❷ SARS [3] _______.

❸ SARS has [4] _______.

❹ The last case of SARS was in 2003.

Reading Comprehension

According to the passage and the following instructions, answer the questions below.

(　　) 1. Which of the following is the picture that shows doctors' advice on how to

擷取訊息 avoid bird flu and SARS?

(A)

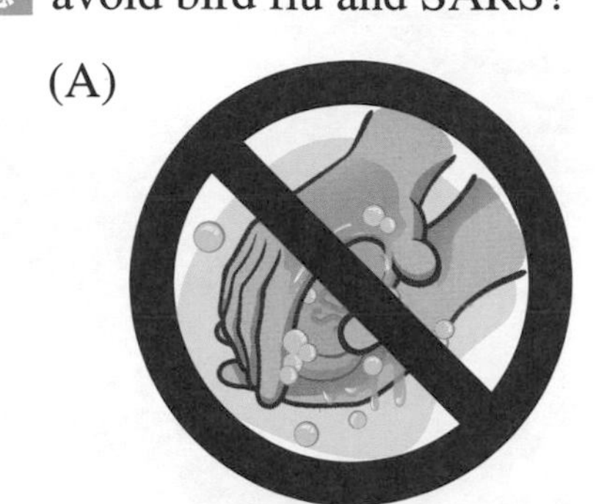

(B)

(C)

(D)

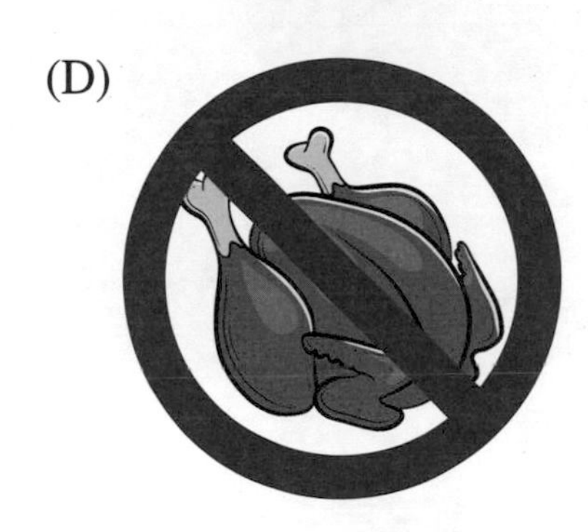

(　　) 2. How is the information about bird flu and SARS organized in the second and

推論整合 third paragraphs?

(A) By pros and cons.　　(B) By cause and effect.

(C) By comparison and contrast.　　(D) By classification.

(　　) 3. Which of the following is **NOT** mentioned in the passage?

擷取訊息 (A) The percentage of people who will die after contracting bird flu.

(B) The consequences of a mutation of bird flu and SARS.

(C) The similarities and differences between the common cold and SARS.

(D) The measures used to avoid being infected with bird flu and SARS.

(　　) 4. Which of the following can be inferred from this passage?

推論整合 (A) Now the bird flu and SARS viruses can be found globally.

(B) Those who suffer from bird flu and SARS face a certain death.

(C) Bird flu is deadlier because it mutates more often than SARS.

(D) Bird flu and SARS viruses attack the victims' respiratory system.

Unit 10

Bugs That Can Eat Plastic?

Let's Go

你有想過毛毛蟲可能成為塑膠垃圾的終結者嗎？而這又會連帶對環境有什麼影響呢？本單元 G.O. 圖搭配 **Sandwich Chart (三明治圖)** 學習，以下為 **Sandwich Chart** 的說明以及示意圖。

說明	示意圖
1. 三明治圖又稱為漢堡圖。 2. 頂層麵包是吸引讀者注意的主題，底層麵包則為總結文章的結論。 3. 中間夾的漢堡肉、生菜和起司為支持細節。一般分為三個觀點：事實、例子、理由等，用以支持文章的主旨。	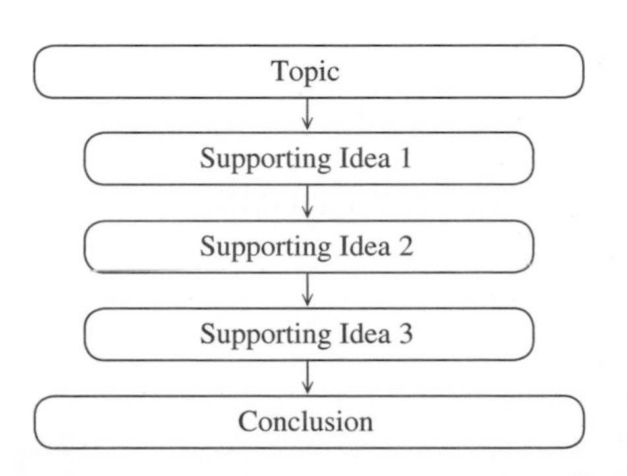

1 A new breakthrough in waste **disposal** may have just been made with the discovery of plastic-eating caterpillars. The discovery was first made by chance when a scientist, an **amateur** beekeeper, found that the larvae of the wax moth had eaten through some of his plastic bags. These caterpillars can eat through polyethylene, which is one of the most common plastics in use. Since this discovery, there has been speculation about using caterpillars to dispose of the plastic that is dumped in our landfills each year. Unfortunately, **breeding** wax moth caterpillars for this purpose comes with a few difficulties.

❷ Each larva can eat about two milligrams 10 of plastic per day. To put this into **perspective**, we would need over one million caterpillars to chew through just one ton of plastic in a year. Considering the UK alone dumps over two million tons of plastic each year, trillions 15 of larvae would be required all year round to make any kind of significant **reduction** in our plastic waste. This is obviously not very **realistic**.

Words for Production

1. disposal *n.* [U] 清除，處理
2. amateur *adj.* 業餘的
3. breed *vt.* 飼養，培育
4. perspective *n.* [U] 客觀判斷力
5. reduction *n.* [U] 減少，縮小，降低
6. realistic *adj.* 實際的

Idioms and Phrases

1. dispose of ... 清除，處理

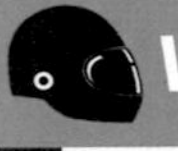

Words for Recognition

1. larva *n.* [C] (*pl. larvae*) 幼蟲
2. polyethylene *n.* [U] 聚乙烯
3. speculation *n.* [U] 推測
4. landfill *n.* [C] 垃圾掩埋場
5. milligram *n.* [C] 毫克
6. trillion *n.* [C] 萬億，兆

20 ❸ The next problem with this proposition is the wax moths themselves. As their name suggests, wax moth larvae feed on the wax honeycombs of beehives. The moths lay from 300 to 600 eggs in a beehive, and the caterpillars that hatch can completely destroy the beehive from within. Huge numbers of honey bees would be
25 under threat if their enemies were allowed to spread. With honey bees so **essential** to our food crops and their populations already at risk, perhaps it is not the best idea to breed trillions of wax moths.

④ This new discovery is not without **promise**, though. Recently, a team of Japanese scientists discovered the bacteria that can eat 30 the plastic used for soda and water bottles. In fact, in 2014, the Indian mealmoth, another kind of wax moth, was already found to carry bacteria in its digestive system that can also break down polyethylene. This suggests that 35 wax moths' ability to break down plastic has more to do with the bacteria they carry than the wax moth caterpillars themselves. Scientists believe that by understanding the way these bacteria break down polyethylene, 40 they can find an alternative way to solve the plastic pollution problem. Maybe in the near future, the plastic pollution will no longer threaten our planet earth.

Words for Production

7. essential *adj.* 極其重要的
8. promise *n.* [U] 獲得成功的跡象

Idioms and Phrases

2. feed on something 以…為食
3. under threat 受到威脅
4. at risk 受到威脅，有危險
5. break down something 使分解，使變化
6. no longer 不再

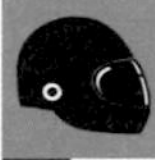

Words for Recognition

7. proposition *n.* [C] 提議，建議
8. bacteria *n. pl.* 細菌
9. digestive *adj.* 消化的

Graphic Organizer

Look at the **Sandwich Chart** and fill in the following blanks with the correct items (A–H) in the box below. The first one has been done for you.

(A) under threat	(B) dispose of	(C) alternative	(D) eat through
(E) realistic	(F) break down	~~(G) discovery~~	(H) feed on

Topic

A new breakthrough in waste disposal has been made with the [1] __(G)__ of plastic-eating caterpillars. There has been speculation about using caterpillars to [2] _______ the plastic waste.

Supporting Idea 1:
the magic that wax moth caterpillars can do to plastic waste

The larvae of the wax moth can [3] _______ the plastic bags.

Supporting Idea 2:
limitations of depending on wax moth caterpillars to clean up plastic waste

❶ Trillions of larvae would be required, and it is not very [4] ________.

❷ Wax moth larvae which [5] _______ the wax honeycombs will destroy the beehives.

❸ Huge numbers of honey bees would be [6] _______ from their enemies.

Supporting Idea 3:
other ways to solve the plastic problem

The bacteria found in the Indian mealmoth's digestive system can [7] _______ polyethylene.

Conclusion

Scientists believe that by understanding the way these bacteria break down the polyethylene, they can find an [8] _______ way to solve the plastic pollution problem.

Reading Comprehension

According to the passage and the following instructions, answer the questions below.

(　　) 1. The following picture is the life cycle of wax moths. Which stage is helpful for

擷取訊息 getting rid of plastic waste?

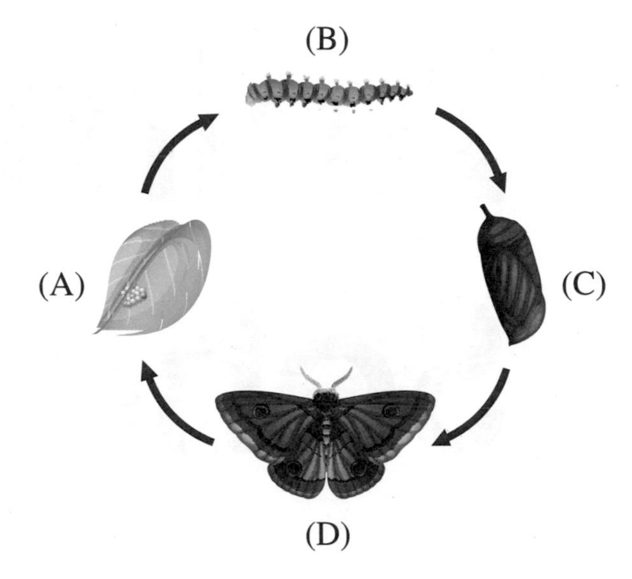

(　　) 2. What does "**This**" in the last sentence of the second paragraph refer to?

評估詮釋 (A) Raising moth larvae to eat plastic.

(B) Dumping two million tons of plastic.

(C) Putting bee populations at risk.

(D) Disposing of plastic waste.

(　　) 3. According to the passage, which of the following statements is true?

擷取訊息 (A) Moth larvae live on honey bees.

(B) Moth caterpillars grow into larvae.

(C) Polyethylene is a common plastic.

(D) Indian mealmoths are not wax moths.

(　　) 4. Which of the following can be inferred from this passage?

推論整合 (A) Large numbers of wax moths will cause more harm than good.

(B) The plastic pollution issue can be solved by studying the behavior of moths.

(C) Indian moths can eat more polyethylene than other wax moths.

(D) The author holds a pessimistic attitude toward the discovery.

The Animal School

Let's Go

動物學校裡面有各種不同的學生，有些擅長游泳、有些擅長跑步。在這間學校裡，動物們在學習上遇到了什麼事情？本單元 G.O. 圖搭配 **Honeycomb Story Map (蜂巢故事圖)** 學習，以下為 **Honeycomb Story Map** 的說明以及示意圖。

說明	示意圖
1. 蜂巢故事圖因形態像蜂巢而得名，通常由五格或七格六角形組成。 2. 蜂巢故事圖常用於分析故事，或協助讀者練習寫故事，例如：五格蜂巢分別是時間、地點、角色、問題與解決法；七格蜂巢可由標題、人物、地點、時間、目的、原因，以及寓意組成。	

❶ Once upon a time, the world's animals had a meeting and determined to **tackle** the problems that troubled the modern world. They built a new school: one that taught running, climbing, flying, and swimming to all of its students, regardless of species.

5 ❷ The duck was an **extraordinary** swimmer, surpassing even his teacher, but barely passed flying and was hopeless when it came to running. Because he was so poor at running, he needed to stay after school to practice. He even had to **drop** his swimming classes to keep up. After a while, his webbed feet had become badly worn 10 from all that practicing. In the end, he was just an average swimmer,

but since he passed running, no one except him cared all that much.

❸ The rabbit began school top in her class at running. However, after hours and hours of make-up classes for swimming, she had a nervous breakdown and had to take time away from school. The squirrel was a talented climber, but became **absolutely** frustrated in flying class. He was forced to begin flying up from the ground rather than flying down from the treetop. As a result, he overworked his muscles and developed terrible cramps. Finally, he got a C in climbing and a D in running.

Words for Production

1. tackle *vt.*
   處理，解決 (難題或局面)
2. extraordinary *adj.*
   卓越的，非凡的
3. drop *vt.*
   停止，放棄 (某種活動)
4. absolutely *adv.* 極其，非常

Idioms and Phrases

1. once upon a time (用於故事的開頭) 從前，很久以前
2. keep up 跟上 (變化、趨勢等)
3. rather than 而不是

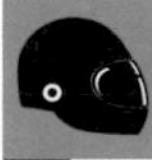

Words for Recognition

1. surpass *vt.* 勝過，優於
2. webbed *adj.* 有蹼的
3. nervous breakdown *n.* [C]
   精神崩潰
4. cramp *n.* [C] 抽筋

30 ❹ The eagle had little regard for the rules. In climbing class, she beat all the other animals to the top of the tree, but not in the way she was supposed to. She was **disciplined harshly**. By the end of the school year, an unusual eel who was a great swimmer and could run, climb, and fly a little had the highest average score in the entire 35 school and graduated with top honors.

❺ However, there were some that never went to school. The prairie dogs **protested** against the lack of digging and burrowing in its **curriculum**. They, along with the groundhogs and the gophers, founded a successful private school for students gifted in digging.

❻ This fable **highlights** the importance of 40 **embracing** individuals' strengths and serves as a reminder that school should not force anyone to meet arbitrary standards at the expense of one's talent. In the same way that an eagle is meant to fly, a singer is meant to 45 sing. A writer writes, and a builder builds.

Words for Production

5. discipline *vt.* 懲罰
6. harshly *adv.* 嚴厲地
7. protest *vt.* 抗議
8. curriculum *n.* [C] (學校等的) 全部課程
9. highlight *vt.* 強調
10. embrace *vt.* 欣然接受、採納 (思想、建議等)

5. prairie dog *n.* [C] 草原犬鼠 (土撥鼠)
6. burrow *vi.* 挖掘 (洞或隧道)
7. groundhog *n.* [C] 美洲旱獺，土撥鼠
8. gopher *n.* [C] 囊地鼠
9. arbitrary *adj.* 主觀武斷的，任意的

Graphic Organizer

Read the story again and fill in the following blanks with the correct items (A–F) in the box below to complete the **Honeycomb Story Map**. The first one has been done for you.

(A) Characters (B) Setting ~~(C) Title~~

(D) Some animals founded another school where students can learn what they want to learn.

(E) It's important to embrace and respect individuals' strengths and talents.

(F) However, no matter how hard the students tried, they couldn't improve the skills they were not good at.

Reading Comprehension

According to the passage and the following instructions, answer the questions below.

(　　) 1. According to the passage, which animal is most likely to have the following

推論整合 report card?

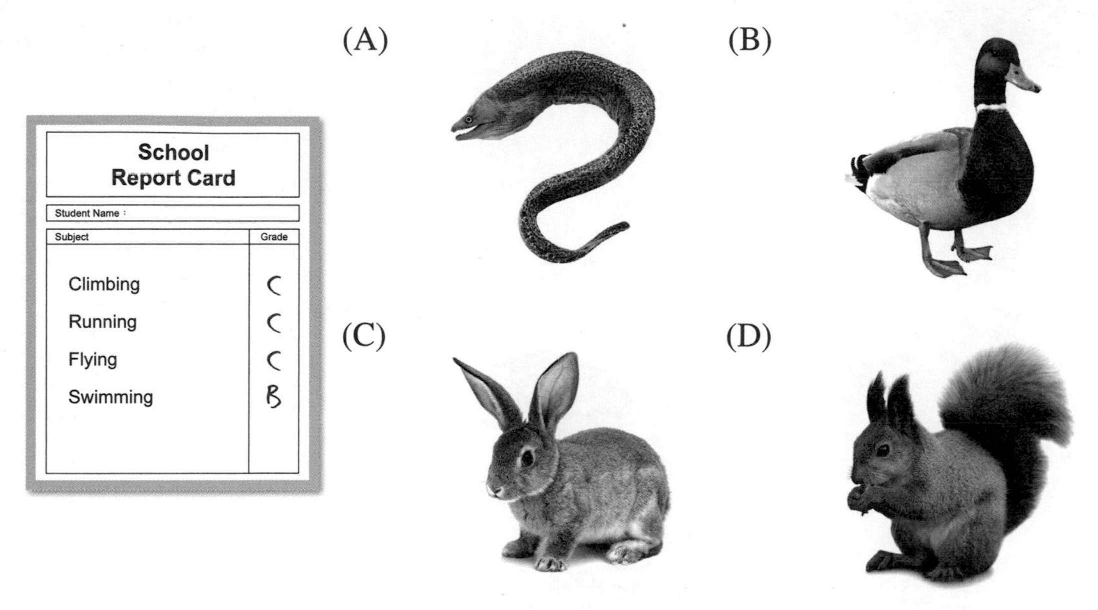

(　　) 2. At the end of the school year, what happened to the animals?

推論整合 (A) They were good at nothing.

(B) They all passed the exams.

(C) They were all injured badly.

(D) They dropped out of school.

(　　) 3. Which of the following about the first school is **NOT** true?

擷取訊息 (A) It forced students to take all the subjects.

(B) It didn't care about students' individual differences.

(C) Students developed their hidden talents with the teachers' help.

(D) Students would be punished if they didn't follow the rules.

(　　) 4. Why was the new school that the prairie dogs founded successful?

評估詮釋 (A) Because it was an expensive private school.

(B) Because it taught talented students only.

(C) Because only gifted students could go to the school.

(D) Because students could develop their talents there.

Unit 12

Dr. Heidegger's Experiment

Let's Go

你可曾聽過長生不老藥水？本單元為一則寓言故事，Heidegger 醫生邀請他的四位老朋友來參與他的開創性實驗，實驗中的藥水究竟有什麼神奇效果？故事中人物在實驗過程中又會發生什麼事呢？本單元 G.O. 圖搭配 **Story Mountain (故事山峰圖)** 學習，以下為 **Story Mountain** 的說明以及示意圖。

說明	示意圖
1. 故事山峰圖根據故事的發展，分為故事開頭 (Beginning 或 Exposition)、情節鋪陳 (Rising Action)、高潮 (Climax)、劇情收尾 (Falling Action)、結局 (Resolution) 等階段。 2. 故事山峰圖主要用來分析記敘文，可增加讀者對故事的了解。	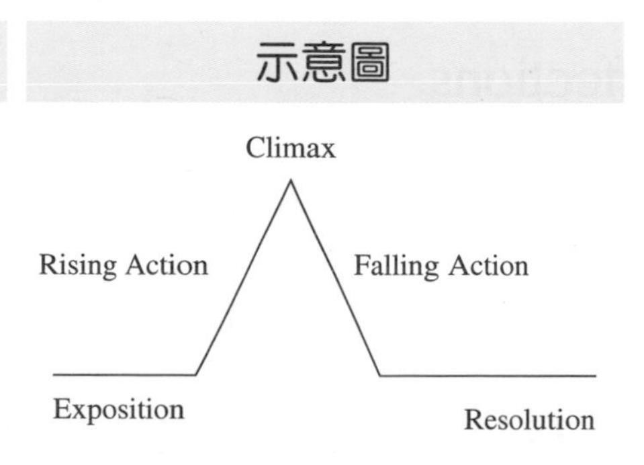

❶ Dr. Heidegger was an eccentric old man who lived alone, spending his days **conducting** experiments or **launching investigations** into his many projects in his **mysterious laboratory**. One day, he invited four of his old friends to take part in a pioneering experiment.

❷ The guests, three men and a woman, were known for having led morally distasteful lives and were now paying the price for their sins in their old ages. Additionally, all three of the men had at one time been the woman's lovers and had fought each other for her **affections**.

❸ Dr. Heidegger took the four of them to his lab and asked them to sit around a table in the middle of the room. In the center of the table was an exquisite vase with a sparkling liquid inside. Then,

Dr. Heidegger presented them with a dry, withered rose and dropped it in the vase. 15 Shortly after the stem touched the liquid, the rose began to change. Soon, it was as if it had been replaced by a freshly-cut rose.

❹ The four guests were shocked but skeptical, thinking it was trickery. The doctor 20 **declared** the water in the vase came from the Fountain of Youth and gave them each a glass. He told his guests that this water could bring back their youth, and that they should remember not to 25 repeat the mistakes they made when they were young. They all agreed.

Words for Production

1. conduct *vt.* 實施，執行
2. launch *vt.* 啟動，從事
3. investigation *n.* [C] 研究，調查
4. mysterious *adj.* 神秘的
5. laboratory *n.* [C] 實驗室
6. affections *n. pl.* 愛情，愛慕
7. declare *vt.* 表明，宣稱

Idioms and Phrases

1. take part (in something) 參與某事
2. at one time 曾經

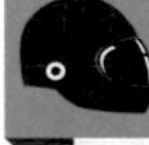

Words for Recognition

1. eccentric *adj.* 古怪的
2. pioneering *adj.* 先驅性的，探索性的
3. distasteful *adj.* 令人反感的
4. exquisite *adj.* 精美的
5. withered *adj.* 枯萎的
6. skeptical *adj.* 懷疑的
7. trickery *n.* [U] 花招，欺騙

30 ❺ Still doubtful, they drank the water, and it was not long before they **transformed** and looked 30 years younger. Feeling a surge of excitement, they drank more. Now they were at the peak of their youth. Bursting with energy, they began **contemplating** all the things they were going to do. However, they were not much different from
35 their former selves. What's more, the men became more and more interested in this now-youthful and beautiful woman and competed for her attention. The situation **deteriorated** into a fight, and in the midst of the conflict, the vase broke, spilling the elixir of youth.

❻ All of a sudden, the rose began to wither and not long after
40 so did the guests. The water's effects were so short-lived that the four felt more hopeless than ever before. Dr. Heidegger learned something about human nature that day. Most people, even if given

the chance to relive their youth, would still make the same mistakes. The four guests learned nothing and resolved to set out in 45 search of the Fountain of Youth.

Words for Production

8. transform *vi.* 改變外觀 (或性質)
9. contemplate *vt.* 考慮，思量
10. deteriorate *vi.* 惡化

Idioms and Phrases

3. in the midst of something 當某事發生時
4. all of a sudden 突然地
5. set out 出發，啟程

Words for Recognition

8. surge *n. sing.* (強烈感情的) 突發
9. elixir *n.* [C] (通常為液體的) 長生不老藥
10. resolve *vi.* 決心，決定

Graphic Organizer

Read the story again and fill in the missing words to complete the **Story Mountain**. The first one has been done for you.

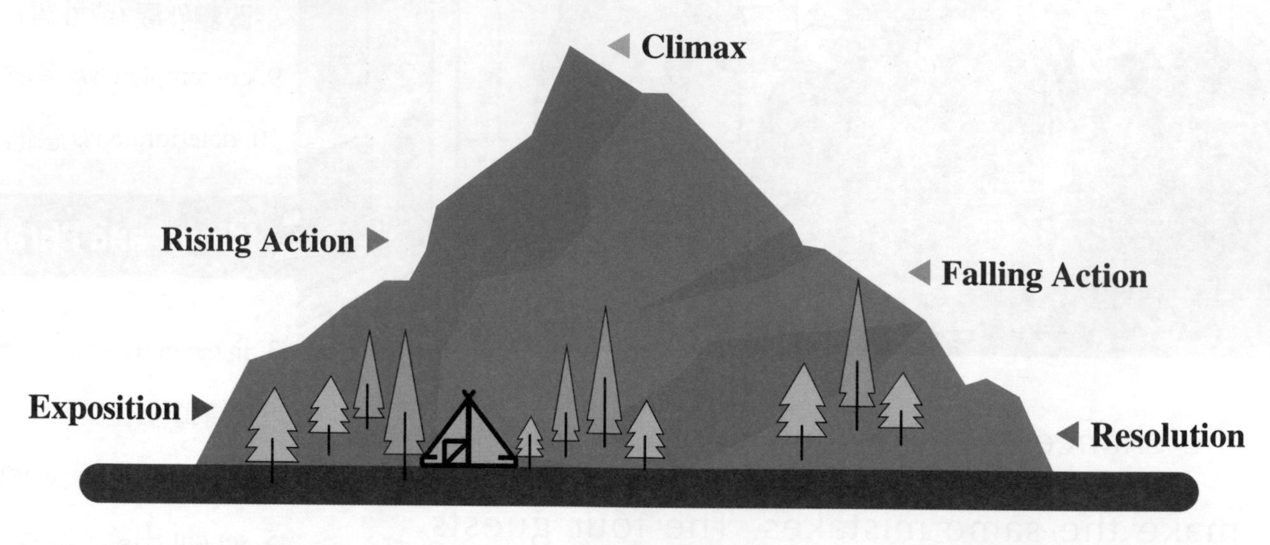

Exposition	Dr. Heidegger invited four of his old friends over to his [1] mysterious laboratory.
Rising Action	Dr. Heidegger dropped a [2] __________ rose into a vase and it became alive again. He claimed that the water came from the Fountain of Youth. Dr. Heidegger gave each of his guests a glass of the [3] __________, warning them not to make the same mistake they did before.
Climax	As Heidegger's guests drank the water, they became young again and got into a [4] __________. Accidentally, they broke the vase.
Falling Action	The four guests became [5] __________ again.
Resolution	Dr. Heidegger learned a [6] __________, but his guests did not.

Reading Comprehension

According to the passage and the following instructions, answer the questions below.

(　　) 1. Which of the following pictures best describes the third paragraph?

擷取訊息 (A)

(B)

(C)

(D)

(　　) 2. What was the four guests' first reaction to Dr. Heidegger's experiment?

擷取訊息 (A) They looked forward to it.

(B) They didn't expect it to work.

(C) They couldn't wait to try it.

(D) They drank the liquid without delay.

(　　) 3. Which of the following sayings is closest in meaning to the theme of the passage?

推論整合

(A) One good turn deserves another.

(B) One man's meat is another's poison.

(C) As you sow, so shall you reap.

(D) A leopard cannot change its spots.

(　　) 4. Which part of the experiment is not mentioned in the story?

評估詮釋 (A) Process.　(B) Result.　(C) Purpose.　(D) Subjects.

GLOSSARY

❶～❻ Word Level
Ⓟ Words for Production
Ⓡ Words for Recognition
▲ Idioms and Phrases

A

absolutely 極其，非常 ❹ U11 Ⓟ
absorb 吸收 ❹ U7 Ⓟ
absurd 荒謬的 ❺ U3 Ⓡ
academic 學術的 ❹ U2 Ⓟ
access 使用的機會 ❹ U7 Ⓟ
accommodations 住處 ❻ U1 Ⓟ
acquire 獲得 ❹ U2 Ⓟ
affections 愛情，愛慕 ❺ U12 Ⓟ
all in all 總之 U9 ▲
all of a sudden 突然地 U12 ▲
allowance 津貼，補助 ❹ U2 Ⓟ
along with U2 ▲
除此之外，還有…
alternative 可供替代的 ❻ U8 Ⓟ
amateur 業餘的 ❹ U10 Ⓟ
application 申請書 ❹ U2 Ⓟ
arbitrary U11 Ⓡ
主觀武斷的，任意的
architecture ❺ U5 Ⓟ
建築設計，建築風格
arise 出現，發生 ❹ U4 Ⓟ
articulate ❻ U3 Ⓡ
明確表達，清楚說明
artificial 人工的 ❹ U1 Ⓟ
as yet 直到現在 U9 ▲
assess 評估，核定 ❻ U2 Ⓡ
at least 至少 U1 ▲
at one time 曾經 U12 ▲
at present 目前，當下 U8 ▲
at risk 受到威脅，有危險 U10 ▲
at the expense of . . . U8 ▲
以…為代價的情況下
authentic 正宗的 ❻ U5 Ⓡ
authority 當局 ❹ U2 Ⓟ

B

bacteria 細菌 U10 Ⓡ
be associated with 與…連結 U7 ▲
behavior 行為，舉止 ❹ U3 Ⓟ
bill 鳥嘴，喙 U4 Ⓡ
biologist 生物學家 U3 Ⓡ
bird flu 禽流感 U9 Ⓡ
bonding ❹ U6 Ⓡ
與…的親密關係聯結
break down something U10 ▲
使分解，使變化
breakthrough ❻ U8 Ⓡ
重大進展，突破
breed 交配繁殖 ❹ U4 Ⓟ
breed 飼養，培育 ❹ U10 Ⓟ
bring . . . to life U5 ▲
使…更有趣，使…更生動
burrow 挖掘 (洞或隧道) U11 Ⓡ
Byzantine 拜占庭帝國的 U5 Ⓡ

C

carbohydrate ❻ U7 Ⓡ
碳水化合物；醣類
catchphrase U3 Ⓡ
時下流行的話語
certified 有合格證書的 ❻ U2 Ⓡ
cetacean 鯨類 U6 Ⓡ
chapel 小教堂 U5 Ⓡ
collision 碰撞，相撞 ❻ U6 Ⓡ
combination 結合 ❹ U6 Ⓟ
come around U9 ▲
(定期發生的事件) 來臨，發生
come to mind U9 ▲
突然記起，想到
communication ❹ U3 Ⓟ
溝通，交流
community 群體 ❹ U5 Ⓟ
compose 組成，構成 ❹ U4 Ⓟ
concentration 專注 ❹ U7 Ⓟ
conduct 實施，執行 ❺ U12 Ⓟ
consumption 食用量 ❻ U7 Ⓟ
contagious ❺ U9 Ⓡ
(疾病) 接觸傳染的
contemplate 考慮，思量 ❺ U12 Ⓟ
contempt 輕視，蔑視 ❺ U1 Ⓡ
contrary 相反的 ❹ U1 Ⓟ
contrast 形成對比 ❹ U4 Ⓟ
contribute 對…有貢獻 ❹ U8 Ⓟ
controversial 具爭議性的 ❻ U8 Ⓟ
convert 轉化 ❺ U7 Ⓟ
convey 表達，傳達 ❹ U3 Ⓟ
cope 處理 ❹ U7 Ⓟ
cosmetics 化妝品 ❻ U8 Ⓡ
craft ❹ U1 Ⓡ
(尤指用手工) 精心製作
cramp 抽筋 ❻ U11 Ⓡ
credentials 資格，資歷 U2 Ⓡ
crucial 至關重要的 ❻ U8 Ⓟ
cuisine 菜餚 ❺ U5 Ⓡ
cultivate 栽種，培育 ❻ U7 Ⓡ
curriculum ❺ U11 Ⓟ
(學校等的) 全部課程
customize 訂製，客製 U3 Ⓡ

D

date back (to . . .) U5 ▲
(時間) 追溯 (到…)
deadly (可能) 致命的 ❻ U9 Ⓡ
declare 表明，宣稱 ❹ U12 Ⓟ
decline 減少，下降 ❻ U4 Ⓟ

including 包括…❹ U2 P

infection 傳染，感染 ❹ U9 P

inflammation 發炎 U7 R

information 資訊 ❹ U6 P

ingredient 材料 ❹ U7 P

inhabitant 居民 ❻ U5 P

innumerable ❺ U6 R
無數的，數不清的

insightful 具洞察力的 U3 R

institution 機構 ❻ U2 P

insulin 胰島素 U7 R

interfere with something U6 A
干擾…，妨礙…

intolerance 過敏 U7 R

invention 發明 ❹ U1 P

investigation 研究，調查 ❹ U12 P

issue 議題 ❺ U8 P

K

keep up U11 A
跟上 (變化、趨勢等)

keep up with 跟上，並駕齊驅 U6 A

keratin U4 R
(羽、髮、角、蹄等的) 角蛋白

L

laboratory 實驗室 ❹ U12 P

landfill 垃圾掩埋場 U10 R

landscape 風景 ❹ U5 P

larva 幼蟲 U10 R

launch 啟動，從事 ❹ U12 P

lifespan 壽命，有效期 U3 R

lizard 蜥蜴 ❺ U4 R

loan 貸款 (需償還) ❹ U2 P

longevity 長壽 ❻ U3 R

Lyra U5 R
里拉琴 (克里特島上的傳統樂器)

M

magnificent ❹ U5 P
壯麗的，宏偉的

make fun of 嘲弄 U3 A

mammal 哺乳動物 ❺ U6 R

mattress 床墊 ❻ U1 R

medication 藥物 ❻ U8 R

Mediterranean 地中海的 U5 R

meme U3 R
模因，模仿傳遞行為 (在網路上迅速傳播的概念、圖像、影像等)

migrate 遷徙 ❻ U4 R

milligram 毫克 U10 R

mocking 嘲弄的 ❺ U3 R

mortality 死亡，死亡數量 U9 R

mosque 清真寺 U5 R

mostly 主要地 ❹ U4 P

multiple 多次的 ❹ U8 P

mutate 突變 U9 R

mysterious 神秘的 ❹ U12 P

N

navigate 導航，確定方向 ❺ U6 R

nervous breakdown U11 R
精神崩潰

no longer 不再 U10 A

notably 尤其，特別 ❺ U1 P

notched V 形切口的 U4 R

notion 觀念 ❺ U1 P

numerous 眾多的 ❹ U7 P

O

obesity 肥胖 U7 R

obtain 獲得 ❻ U2 P

offspring 子女，後代 ❻ U4 R

on the contrary U3 A
正好相反的是

on the one hand . . . on the other hand . . . U8 A
一方面…另一方面…

once in a while 偶爾地 U6 A

once upon a time U11 A
(用於故事的開頭) 從前，很久以前

option 選修課 ❻ U2 R

Ottoman 鄂圖曼帝國的 U5 R

overexposure 過度暴露於… U7 P

P

pair off 出雙入對，配對 U4 A

paragraph 段落 ❹ U3 P

pay . . . a visit 拜訪… U4 A

percent 百分之… ❹ U8 P

perspective 客觀判斷力 ❻ U10 P

phenomenon 現象 ❹ U6 P

picturesque 優美的 ❻ U5 R

pioneering ❹ U12 R
先驅性的，探索性的

plague 使受折磨，困擾 ❺ U7 R

pod U6 R
(海豚或鯨等海洋動物的) 一群

polyethylene 聚乙烯 U10 R

possess 擁有 ❹ U5 P

potential 可能性 ❺ U6 P

prairie dog U11 R
草原犬鼠 (土撥鼠)

prevention 預防 ❹ U9 P

production 生產 ❹ U7 P

productive 有效益的 ❹ U1 P

proficiency 精熟程度 ❻ U2 R

promise 獲得成功的跡象 U10 P

propagation 傳播，宣傳 U3 R

proposition 提議，建議 U10 R

protein 蛋白質 ❹ U4 P

protest 抗議 ❹ U11 Ⓟ
psychological 心理的 ❹ U7 Ⓟ

R

rather than 而不是 U11 ▲
read up on something U2 ▲
(為了得到有關資訊) 廣泛閱讀…
realistic 實際的 ❹ U10 Ⓟ
reduction ❹ U10 Ⓟ
減少，縮小，降低
regardless of 不管，不論 U3 ▲
regulate ❹ U4 Ⓟ
控制、調節 (溫度)
regulate ❹ U8 Ⓟ
(用規則條例) 約束，管理
relatively 相對地 ❹ U7 Ⓟ
relevant 緊密相關的 ❻ U3 Ⓟ
reliability 可信度 U8 🅁
remarkable 引人注目的 ❹ U4 Ⓟ
research 調查，探索 ❹ U2 Ⓟ
resistance 抵抗 ❹ U7 Ⓟ
resolve 決心，決定 ❹ U12 🅁
respiratory 呼吸的 U9 🅁
result in 導致，結果造成 U6 ▲
rigidly 僵硬、僵直的 ❺ U1 Ⓟ
roam 徜徉 ❺ U6 🅁

S

sarcastic 嘲諷的 U3 🅁
SARS (= severe acute respiratory syndrome) U9 🅁
嚴重急性呼吸道症候群
secure 設法得到 ❺ U2 Ⓟ
set out 出發，啟程 U12 ▲
severely 嚴重地 ❹ U6 Ⓟ
sewage 汙水 U1 🅁
skeptical 懷疑的 ❻ U12 🅁
sociable 善於社交的 ❻ U4 🅁
sophisticated 複雜的 ❻ U3 Ⓟ
species 物種 ❹ U4 Ⓟ
spectacular 壯麗的 ❻ U5 Ⓟ
speculation 推測 U10 🅁
spike 猛增，急升 ❻ U7 🅁
standardized 標準化的 U2 🅁
staple 主要的 ❻ U7 🅁
strain (疾病的) 類型，品種 ❺ U9 Ⓟ
strand 使滯留、擱淺 ❻ U6 Ⓟ
strikingly 顯著地 U4 🅁
Student and Exchange Visitor Program (SEVP) U2 🅁
國際學生和交流訪客計劃
substantial 大量的 ❺ U4 Ⓟ
surge (強烈感情的) 突發 ❺ U12 🅁
surpass 勝過，優於 ❻ U11 🅁
surroundings 環境 ❹ U6 Ⓟ
sweltering 酷熱難耐的 U4 🅁
symptom 症狀 ❻ U7 Ⓟ

T

tackle ❺ U11 Ⓟ
處理，解決 (難題或局面)
take part (in something) U12 ▲
參與某事
take up something U1 ▲
佔用 (時間)
tavern 小酒館 ❺ U5 🅁
the Industrial Revolution U1 🅁
工業革命 (18–19 世紀)
the Internet 網際網路 U3 Ⓟ
the Middle Ages 中世紀 U1 🅁
the Renaissance U1 🅁
文藝復興時期 (14–16 世紀)
thesis 論點 U3 🅁
toxin 毒素 U6 🅁
transfer 傳染，轉移 (疾病) ❹ U9 Ⓟ
transform ❹ U12 Ⓟ
改變外觀 (或性質)
transmission 傳播，傳染 ❻ U9 Ⓟ
transmit 傳播，傳染 ❻ U9 Ⓟ
trickery 花招，欺騙 U12 🅁
trillion 萬億，兆 U10 🅁
Turkish 土耳其的 U5 🅁

U

under threat 受到威脅 U10 ▲
uninterrupted 不間斷的 U1 🅁
unique 獨特的 ❹ U5 Ⓟ
unsanitary U1 🅁
不衛生的，不潔的
uplifting 令人振奮的 U7 🅁

V

vaccine 疫苗 ❻ U8 🅁
Venetian 威尼斯式的 U5 🅁
version 版本 ❻ U3 Ⓟ
vibrant 鮮豔的 U4 🅁
virus 病毒 ❹ U9 Ⓟ
visa 簽證 ❺ U2 🅁

W

wash something up U6 🅁
把…沖到陸地上
webbed 有蹼的 ❸ U11 🅁
whereas ❺ U9 Ⓟ
(用以比較兩個事實) 然而，但是
wholesome ❺ U5 🅁
有益的 (生理和心理層面皆是)
withdrawal symptoms U7 🅁
脫癮症狀
withered 枯萎的 ❺ U12 🅁
without a doubt 毫無疑問地 U5 ▲

國家圖書館出版品預行編目資料

英文閱讀GO, GO, GO!／應惠蕙編著.——二版一刷.
——臺北市：三民，2023
面；　公分.——（Reading Power系列）

ISBN 978-957-14-7595-0（平裝）
1. 英語 2. 讀本

805.18　　111021009

英文閱讀 GO, GO, GO!

作　者　應惠蕙
審 訂 者　Peter John Wilds

發 行 人　劉振強
出 版 者　三民書局股份有限公司
地　址　臺北市復興北路 386 號 (復北門市)
　　　　臺北市重慶南路一段 61 號 (重南門市)
電　話　(02)25006600
網　址　三民網路書店 https://www.sanmin.com.tw

出版日期　初版一刷 2020 年 2 月
　　　　　二版一刷 2023 年 11 月
書籍編號　S802910
I S B N　978-957-14-7595-0

三民書局

Reading Power 系列

★ 108 課綱、全民英檢中級適用
★ 可搭配 108 課綱加深加廣選修課程及多元選修課程

英文閱讀 G.O., G.O., G.O.!

(二版)

翻譯與解析

應惠蕙 編著
Peter John Wilds 審訂

文章架構圖像化！

第一本中文詳解圖形組織圖 (G.O.) 的英文閱讀書

三民書局

Graphic Organizer

2. A 3. D 4. B 5. F 6. C

Reading Comprehension

1. B 2. C 3. D 4. A

我們都是怎麼睡覺的

研究指出，我們並沒有獲得充足的優質睡眠，這其實不讓人意外。我們的生活充滿壓力而且現代人又常常熬夜。跟普遍認知相反的是，一般認為過去的人們生活較為刻苦但生活作息比較均衡，其實，他們的睡眠品質沒有比我們好到哪裡去。

目前所知最早的床，出現於西元前八千年左右，而這所謂的床，不過是把草和柔軟的植物塞進洞穴牆壁上的凹洞裡。事實上，這種床的大小只足夠讓人們以胎兒的姿勢入睡，絕對不是什麼五星級的住宿體驗。

隨著文明進步，睡覺這方面並沒有太多改善。羅馬人輕視睡眠的必要性，因為睡眠所佔用的時間，他們寧願花在更有生產價值的活動上，像是闢路或是蓋橋。羅馬人偏好睡在簡樸的房間裡，小床是木製床架，床墊則是稻草填充而成的，而且在黎明之前就早早起床了。

到了中世紀，人們的睡眠品質似乎變得更差了，最主要的原因在於讓人幾乎無法忍受的惡臭味。當時，人們缺乏適當的汙水排水系統，又生活在不衛生的環境裡，並且持續有火在燒。糞便、汙水與濃煙的味道混在一起，肯定相當難聞。此外，為了取暖，家人們會擠在一起睡，可說是沒有什麼隱私可言。

文藝復興時期，人們的睡眠品質開始提升，這個時期的人們在床架上架設繩索來支撐床墊，並降低床的硬度。同個時期的中國正值明朝，也開始精心打造大型的裝飾床架，這些華麗的床不只有睡覺的用途，白天時也會用來娛樂訪客。

在工業革命時代，人造光源的發明戲劇性地改變了人們睡眠的方式。工業革命前，人們會先睡四個小時，在半夜醒來做雜務，然後再回到床上睡四個小時。但是，隨著燈泡的發明，人們在日落之後不需要直接去睡覺。相反的是，人們開始和朋友閒晃到很晚。直到 1920 年代，人們才採取連續八小時的睡眠模式。近年來，為了健康考量，睡眠研究人員也建議八小時的睡眠模式。

雖然我們的睡眠習慣並不是最健康的，但至少大部分的人在夜晚進入夢鄉的時候，頭頂上都有遮風避雨的屋頂，床也溫暖又舒適。

1.	下面哪一張圖片最可能是一萬年前的床？	**擷取訊息**
	(A) 放在洞穴中間地上草堆做的床。	
✓	(B) 草堆床塞在洞穴牆邊的小凹洞。	
	(C) 空房間中的地上鋪著床墊。	
	(D) 戶外的草地上。	

解析：
根據文章第二段，最早的床出現在西元前八千年，是由塞了草、花，在洞穴牆邊凹洞而成的床。故選 (B)。

2.	這篇文章主要講述的是什麼？	**推論整合**
	(A) 人們怎麼看待睡眠這件事。	
	(B) 床是什麼做的。	
✓	(C) 為什麼人們總睡不好。	
	(D) 人們在閒暇時候都做些什麼。	

解析：
根據文章第一段，以前的人的睡眠品質不比現代人好，後來一直到文藝復興時期，人們的睡眠品質才有所改善。最後一直到 1920 年代，人們才能連續睡上八小時。由此可見本文主要說明為何以前的人睡得不好。故選 (C)。

3.	關於床演進的歷史，本篇文章所提供的資訊是以何種方式呈現的？	評估詮釋
	(A) 品質的順序。	
	(B) 空間的順序。	
	(C) 重要性的順序。	
✓	(D) 時間的順序。	

解析：

本文從第二段起，一直到文末係按照時間順序，從古到今排列段落內容。故選 (D)。

4.	下列哪個選項可由文章推論出來？	推論整合
✓	(A) 睡覺的場所與休息的品質息息相關。	
	(B) 隨著時間演進，人們睡眠的品質變好了。	
	(C) 從文藝復興時期開始，人們花在睡眠上的時間變多了。	
	(D) 因為日落而息，過去的人們睡得比較好。	

解析：

(A) 文中提到中世紀衛生不良影響睡眠，然而文藝復興時期，因為床的改良，人們睡眠有改善，因此可推知，睡眠地點影響人們休息的品質。故選 (A)。
(B) 以前人們睡眠品質不佳，但到了文藝復興有所改善，不過工業革命後卻又變差了。故 (B) 為非。
(C) 工業革命後，因為燈泡的發明，人們入夜後待在外面的時間變多了，因此並未睡得更多。故 (C) 為非。
(D) 第一段即指出以前的人並未睡得比現代人好。故 (D) 為非。

Unit 2

Graphic Organizer

2. Second/Next/Besides/Furthermore/In addition/Also
3. After/Once
4. Furthermore/Besides/In addition/Also/Next
5. After/Once
6. the next stage
7. Finally/Lastly/Last but not least

Reading Comprehension

1. D 2. C 3. A 4. D

做個美國留學生

美國是世界上最熱門的留學地點之一，這是有原因的，它擁有世界頂尖的學術機構與超過四千所一流大學，因此，許多在科學、科技、商業與藝術上創新的進展，最早都是在美國的大學開始發展，也就不足為奇了。一旦你決定去美國留學是正確的選擇，為了做好準備並具備入學資格，你必須經歷下列五個步驟。

要成為美國留學生的第一步，就是先調查自己有哪幾間學校可選擇。那些讓你感興趣的大學應該要提供你希望修習的課程，除了位於理想的地點外，也應取得「國際學生和交流訪客計畫」(Student and Exchange Visitor Program，簡稱 SEVP) 的認證。

下一步是確保資金無虞，美國政府並沒有提供國際留學生貸款、補助金或獎學金，但是，如果你或你的家庭沒辦法負擔這筆開銷，可以透過其他管道取得資金，可能的補助來源包括：你自己國家的教育組織、美國學術機構、私人基金會與企業，以及美國官方的交換學生計畫等。

獲得資金之後，就可以開始申請理想的大學了。入學許可是由你想要就讀的機構直接審核，此外，你可能需要報考某個標準化測驗，以及托福這類的英文水平測驗。

一旦你被 SEVP 認證的大學錄取，一定要申請學生簽證。要拿到它，你會需要填寫一個線上表格，並和國內的美國大使館安排面談時間。

最後，你必須做好在美國生活的準備，確保自己知悉當地法律、津貼還有簽證身分在移民、就業與稅金上的限制；研究如何獲得駕照，或許也可以開始搜尋以英文作為第二語言的相關課程；多了解美國的節日與廣泛閱讀一些有用的資訊。祝你好運！

1.	以下什麼東西不是在申請美國大學時需要準備的？	**擷取訊息**
	(A) 托福成績單。	
	(B) 學生簽證。	
	(C) 美國大使館預約面談的線上表單。	
✓	(D) 駕照。	

解析：

駕照是為了方便在美國生活，並非申請大學必須的文件。故選 (D)。

2.	這篇文章的目的是什麼？	**推論整合**
	(A) 鼓勵讀者去美國念書。	
	(B) 幫助讀者取得美國大學的入學許可。	
✓	(C) 清楚說明申請美國大學的流程。	
	(D) 告訴讀者申請美國大學有多麼困難。	

解析：

本文主要目的在說明申請美國大學的步驟，作者並未明確鼓勵讀者赴美就讀，亦未幫讀者取得入學許可，故選 (C)。

3.	根據文章，下列哪一段敘述為真？	**擷取訊息**
✓	(A) 美國大學對於學術研究有很大的貢獻。	
	(B) 因為能透過線上申請，所以美國大學很熱門。	
	(C) 美國政府提供外國學生資金補助。	
	(D) 了解美國的法律是國際學生最不該做的一件事。	

解析：

(A) 第一段說明美國大學在科學、科技、商業與藝術方面有創新的進步，證明其在學術研究上有很大的貢獻，故選 (A)。
(B) 第一段指出美國大學受歡迎的原因係其創新的進步，與線上申請無關。故 (B) 為非。
(C) 第三段明確指出美國政府不提供國際生貸款、助學金或獎學金。故 (C) 為非。
(D) the last thing one should do 最不需要做的事。

4.	下列何者可能是一名學生沒辦法在美國大學就讀的原因？	**推論整合**
	(A) 沒有拿到獎學金。	
	(B) 沒有在托福測驗獲得高分。	
	(C) 不太會講美式英文。	
✓	(D) 沒有美國學生簽證。	

解析：

(A) 第三段提出雖沒有獎學金仍有其他方法獲得資金。故 (A) 為非。
(B) TOEFL 成績必要，但文中並未提出需要高分，最後一段提出可上英文為外語的課程。故 (B) 為非。
(C) 美式英文說得不太好也可修習英文為外語的課程。故 (C) 為非。
(D) 第五段指出學生簽證是必要的，沒有就無法赴美就讀。故選 (D)。

Graphic Organizer

2. H　3. E　4. C　5. A　6. F　7. G　8. D

Reading Comprehension

1. B　2. B　3. C　4. D

模因的病毒式傳播

每個人都曾在某個時刻些時候看過「網路模因」，也就是社群媒體上如野火般傳播的那些搞笑文字、影像、流行語或圖檔。「模因」這個詞最初是由演化生物學家 Richard Dawkins 在其 1976 年出版的著作《自私的基因》中所創造的，他將模因描述為一種文化傳播的形式、迅速從一個人的腦中傳遞到另一個人腦中的思想。這些思想可以很淺顯，也可以很複雜，它們大多以誇張的方式來模仿人類的行事風格。

美國喜劇演員 Gene Wilder 的一張圖檔，就是一個很好的模因例子。於電影《歡樂糖果屋》飾演 Willy Wonka 的他，在圖中用嘲諷的神情，假裝對某件事物很感興趣，這張圖常和「多告訴我一點」的諷刺標語放在一起，用來嘲弄某人對某事的了解程度。這些運用相同圖檔與相似標語的模因，通常被客製化來傳達不同主題下的相同概念。

為什麼模因會那麼受歡迎，又散播地如此迅速呢？模因之所以為模因，是因為它們容易辨識與理解，它們能清楚且有效地傳達好幾個段落、甚至幾篇文章才能闡述的概念。此外，網路的即時傳播性也讓模因在短時間內觸及數百萬人。一個模因所傳達的概念可以很簡單，也能很深入且富有意義，但是，不管表達的是什麼概念，要達成病毒般的爆紅效果，仰賴的是模因的執行成果，如：幽默程度、關聯性、是否引人注目、荒謬感和明確度。

不論一個模因是多麼精闢或多麼巧妙，最終都會過時、消逝。每個模因的生命週期各不相同，它的壽命取決於許多因素。許多模因都只是網路上的一窩蜂，有些很快就過氣，有些則能持續被使用達數年之久。

乍看之下，比起文字，模因所能傳達的內涵似乎較為淺白。但事實恰好相反，就像是一圖勝千言一樣，模因也具備相同的效果，此外，它還蘊含了一個中心論點，而且幾乎可以立刻傳遍全球。

1.	第三段的「viral」這個字最有可能是什麼意思？	**評估詮釋**
	(A) 交錯。	
✓	(B) 擴散。	
	(C) 緊縮。	
	(D) 循環。	

解析：
從第一段模因如野火般擴散，到第二段模因可根據主題而使用類似但不盡相同的文字在同樣的畫面，可知 viral 是擴展的意思。故選 (B)。

2.	根據文章，下列哪個關於 Willy Wonka 模因的論述為真？	**推論整合**
	(A) Willy Wonka 所說的話都是真心的。	
✓	(B) 圖片上的文字可根據不同情況置換。	
	(C) 如果讀者想要知道更多，他們可以使用此模因。	
	(D) 此模因的目的在於取笑某人的臉部表情。	

解析：
(A) 第二段指出 Willy Wonka 的表情，假裝感興趣，因此他說的話不真誠。故 (A) 為非。
(B) 第二段最後一句指出，模因是使用同一張圖片，針對不同主題設計出類似但不同的文字。故選 (B)。

(C) 根據文章第二段，此模因並非真誠想多了解，因此如果讀者想多了解事情，不應使用此模因來表示。故 (C) 為非。
(D) 此模因並非在嘲笑別人的表情，而是以嘲諷的表情假裝對事情感興趣。故 (D) 為非。

3.	下列何者不是模因的特性？ **擷取訊息**
	(A) 誇大人們所做的事。
	(B) 傳播迅速。
✓	(C) 改變人們的行為。
	(D) 包含圖像與文字。

解析：

(A) 第一段最後一行指出，模因會以誇張的方式複製人類的行為。故 (A) 為對。
(B) 模因可快速在人與人之間擴散，文章第三段並說明原因。故 (B) 為對。
(C) 文中提到模因會因主題而做些許改變，但並未提到會改變人類的行為。故 (C) 為非，為本題正解。
(D) 第二段最後一句提到，模因利用同一圖片，但為不同主題訂製不同的文字說明，以表達相同的概念。故 (D) 為對。

4.	下列何者不曾在文章中提及？ **推論整合**
	(A) 模因的預期壽命。
	(B) 模因的例子。
	(C) 模因這個字的來源。
✓	(D) 模因的優點與缺點。

解析：

(A) 第四段指出，模因有些很快就過氣，有些則能持續被使用達數年之久。故 (A) 為對。
(B) 第二段為模因的例子。故 (B) 為對。
(C) 第一段有提到模因這個字的由來。故 (C) 為對。
(D) 文中並未提到模因的優缺點，故 (D) 為非，為本題正解。

Graphic Organizer

2. beak 3. tropical 4. forests 5. sociable 6. breed 7. fruits 8. digest 9. hunted 10. decoration

Reading Comprehension

1. C 2. B 3. D 4. A

大嘴一族：巨嘴鳥

以滑稽大嘴聞名的巨嘴鳥是世上最受歡迎的鳥類之一，其中，體型最大且最具代表性的托哥巨嘴鳥可以長到六十三公分高，重達六百二十公克。不同亞種的巨嘴鳥，羽毛顏色也不相同，但大多以黑色為主，參雜幾抹白色、紅色、紫色與黃色羽毛點綴其中。舉例來說，托哥巨嘴鳥有著黑色的身軀，與白色的喉嚨及巨大鮮豔的黃橙色鳥喙形成強烈的對比。

巨嘴鳥引人注目的鳥嘴不管是長度或寬度都很巨大，有些巨嘴鳥的鳥喙甚至超過自己身長的一半，但是實際重量比看起來要輕得多。巨嘴鳥的鳥喙外層由角蛋白組成；內部則是骨質纖維，骨質纖維的結構中含有大量氣囊。鳥喙的邊緣有著 V 形缺口，方便巨嘴鳥用來剝皮去殼以及享用大型水果。巨嘴鳥的鳥喙也能有效調節身體溫度，在酷暑難耐的熱帶雨林中，此功能極為重要。

巨嘴鳥生活在南美洲的熱帶與亞熱帶地區，範圍從南墨西哥延伸到北阿根廷。牠們大多居住在有著巨大古樹的森林裡，這些巨樹的洞穴大到足以讓牠們繁衍後代。牠們很少飛往別處，也不遷徙，通常在樹木間是以跳躍而非飛行的方式移動。

至於巨嘴鳥的習性，牠們非常善於社交，一生中大部分時間都在至多有二十隻同伴的群體裡生活。其他時間，牠們會在交配季節成雙成對行動以繁殖後代，然後帶著孩子回到原本的群體中。巨嘴鳥以水果為主食，但是如果有機會，牠們也會吃昆蟲、小型的蜥蜴與鳥類。吃下水果後，牠們大約需要三十五分鐘的時間消化，直到消化完成之前不會再進食，而這段時間就被牠們用來從事玩耍、追逐與互相呼叫等社交活動。

因其獨特的外觀，巨嘴鳥是鳥類中較為知名的種類之一。傳統上，人類獵捕牠們當作食物，或作為寵物豢養，羽毛與鳥喙則被拿來作為裝飾。在某些地區，找到巨嘴鳥巢穴的人便能獲得其所有權，可出售巢中所有的鳥。雖然巨嘴鳥並不是瀕危物種，但據估計，牠們的數量正在減少中。遺憾的是，很多遊客會購買由巨嘴鳥鳥喙、鳥羽等製成的禮品。因此，如果你有機會拜訪牠們，請確保你只帶走有著牠們美麗身影的照片就好。

1.	下面哪一張圖比較像是巨嘴鳥的棲地？	**擷取訊息**
	(A) 灌木叢。	
	(B) 針葉林。	
✓	(C) 大樹 (樹幹上有樹洞)。	
	(D) 水筆仔 (生在水中)。	

解析：

根據第三段巨嘴鳥居住在大型老樹樹幹的樹洞裡，故選 (C)。

2.	什麼造成了巨嘴鳥的數量正在減少？	**推論整合**
	(A) 牠們善於社交的行為。	
✓	(B) 牠們獨特的外觀。	
	(C) 牠們過重的黑色鳥喙。	
	(D) 牠們特殊的獵食習慣。	

解析：

(A) 文中並未提到善於社交導致巨嘴鳥數量減少。故 (A) 為非。

(B) 最後一段提到人們喜歡用其羽毛和喙作裝飾品，因此數量減少。故選 (B)。

(C) 第一段提到巨嘴鳥的喙是亮橘色的。故 (C) 為非。

(D) 文中提到巨嘴鳥會被獵捕，但並未提其獵捕習慣。故 (D) 為非。

3.	下列哪一個敘述是作者的想法？	**評估詮釋**
	(A) 巨嘴鳥的鳥喙是以角蛋白與骨質纖維組成。	
	(B) 巨嘴鳥的喙可以幫助調節體溫。	
	(C) 巨嘴鳥以群聚的型態居住在南美洲的樹洞裡。	
✓	(D) 人們應該避免購買巨嘴鳥的羽毛與鳥喙。	

解析：

(A) (B) (C) 均為事實，(D) 最後一段最後一句作者呼籲讀者不要購買由巨嘴鳥製作的商品。

4.	我們可以從文章中學到什麼？	**擷取訊息**
✓	(A) 巨嘴鳥的鳥喙有孔洞。	
	(B) 巨嘴鳥的大嘴讓牠們看起來很笨拙。	
	(C) 巨嘴鳥需要大約一個半小時來消化昆蟲。	
	(D) 由於現在巨嘴鳥數量變少，獵捕與販賣牠們是違法的行為。	

解析：

(A) 第二段提到巨嘴鳥的喙有許多氣囊，囊袋即為中空的部分。故選 (A)。

(B) 文中並未提到大嘴讓巨嘴鳥看起來笨重。故 (B) 為非。

(C) 巨嘴鳥需要三十五分鐘消化水果，且並非昆蟲。故 (C) 為非。

(D) 今日巨嘴鳥雖然較少，但獵捕販售並非違法。故 (D) 為非。

Graphic Organizer

2. G　3. D　4. A　5. E　6. H　7. C　8. F

Reading Comprehension

1. B　2. D　3. A　4. C

克里特島：地中海的寶石

克里特島是希臘最大、最南端的島嶼，以多樣化的景色聞名。它擁有獨特的文化，使它與該國其他地區截然不同。克里特島人的驕傲其來有自，他們擁有豐富的歷史、美味的食物和生氣蓬勃的文化，還被如畫一般的地中海美景所環繞。

無疑地，吸引遊客前來克里特島度假的首要原因是美麗多樣的景色，它的北側有白色沙灘、南側有壯麗的海岸線、中部則有廣闊的峽谷、深遠的河谷與被雪覆蓋的高山等，克里特島確實什麼都有。

島民朝氣蓬勃的文化使得這座島嶼更加美麗，也可以說，是克里特島的人民賦予了它生命。無論是用里拉琴等傳統樂器即興演奏的音樂家，或日常相約在咖啡館聊天的人們，這些克里特島居民似乎過著十分有益於身心的生活，他們個性務實，居住在緊密連結的社區裡。

有著豐富的文化，克里特島當然也有著令人驚豔的美食。在克里特島，無論是小鎮的餐廳或小酒館所提供的食物，都是自家生產，包括起司、肉類、橄欖油、葡萄酒等，海鮮也是由店家親自出海捕撈。無論你在島嶼的任何角落，都可以找到新鮮、道地、用心烹調、充滿熱情的在地美食。

克里特島擁有豐富的歷史，最早的歷史紀錄可回溯至西元前兩千年。它是歐洲最古老的文明——米諾恩文明的起源地，在米諾恩文明時期，克諾索斯王宮是當時最宏偉的建築。從那時候開始，歷史以許多形式在克里特島的建築上留下痕跡，例如：拜占庭風格的禮拜堂與教堂、威尼斯人建造的城市與堡壘、土耳其式的澡堂與鄂圖曼時期的清真寺等。

世界上沒有幾個地方，能宣稱自己擁有如此豐富的歷史、多樣的自然景觀、美味的料理與務實、富有活力的人民，但克里特島肯定是其中之一。

1.	根據文章，下列哪張圖會是克里特島的旅行指南？	**擷取訊息**
	(A) 1. 享用當地美食。 2. 上烹飪課程。 3. 拜訪歷史遺跡。 4. 探索並享受深谷風景。	
✓	(B) 1. 欣賞多樣化的景觀。 2. 參加歷史探訪行程。 3. 品嚐當地自產料理。 4. 體驗充滿活力的生活方式。	
	(C) 1. 和當地居民聊天。 2. 展開環島自行車之旅。 3. 嘗試水上活動。 4. 拜訪歷史博物館。	
	(D) 1. 享受多樣化的風景。 2. 沉浸在異國文化中。 3. 欣賞地中海景觀。 4. 體驗步調快速的生活。	

解析：

(A) 文中並未提到有烹飪課。故 (A) 為非。
(B) 文中提到克里特島有多樣的風景、豐富的歷史文明，當地居民朝氣蓬勃，並自產食物。故選 (B)。
(C) 文中並未提到騎腳踏車環島，可參觀歷史遺跡，但並未提到歷史博物館。故 (C) 為非。
(D) 克里特島的人生活有朝氣充滿熱情，推論生活步調應該不是非常快速。故 (D) 為非。

2.	第一段中的「vibrant」是什麼意思？	**評估詮釋**
	(A) 暴力的。	
	(B) 晃動的。	
	(C) 古老的。	
✓	(D) 有活力的。	

解析：
由第三段 bring the island to life 及最後一段的 lively，得知 vibrant 意思應是「有活力的」。故選 (D)。

3.	根據文章，下列敘述何者正確？	**擷取訊息**
✓	(A) 克里特島豐富的建築是受到其長遠且多樣化的歷史影響。	
	(B) 因為觀光業發達，克里特島的人都很富有。	
	(C) 在希臘，克里特島優美的地中海景觀是獨一無二的。	
	(D) 克里特島人忙著經營餐廳維生。	

解析：
(A) 由第五段克里特島有豐富的歷史建築，為多種文明匯集地，得知 (A) 為對。故選 (A)。
(B) 文中並未提到觀光業讓克里特島居民富有。故 (B) 為非。
(C) 第一段提到克里特島的文化與希臘其他地方不同，並非指地中海風景。故 (C) 為非。
(D) 文中並未提到克里特島人以開餐廳維生。故 (D) 為非。

4.	這篇文章最有可能出現在哪裡？	**推論整合**
	(A) 即時新聞報導。	
	(B) 米其林餐廳指南。	
✓	(C) 旅遊指南。	
	(D) 歷史課本。	

解析：
本文應在旅遊指南、百科全書或國家地理雜誌之類書籍中出現。故選 (C)。

Unit 6

Graphic Organizer

2. toxins 3. injury 4. collisions 5. errors
6. unfamiliar 7. bonding 8. stranded

Reading Comprehension

1. D 2. A 3. B 4. D

鯨魚為什麼擱淺

鯨魚是海洋中的大型哺乳類動物，也是地球上最大的動物。牠們在海洋中遨遊、遷徙數千公里之遠、和群體成員一起獵食及社交。然而，碩大的體型並不能保證牠們的安全。鯨魚最主要的死因之一就是擱淺，這看似難以置信，但鯨魚確實偶爾會讓自己受困沙灘。這種現象稱為「鯨豚擱淺」，指的就是鯨魚和海豚自己受困於淺灘上。儘管很難知道鯨魚擱淺的確切原因，專家找出了一些因素，無論是單獨發生或交互影響，都可能造成鯨魚擱淺。

首先，許多擱淺於沙灘上的鯨魚不是年老就是生病了。這些鯨魚會擱淺，是因為牠們跟不上鯨群的速度、或者不夠強壯，無法抵擋海洋的浪潮將牠們拉到岸邊。鯨魚生病或身體不好的原因有很多，例如：臨時的自然疾病、毒素與重金屬的累積，以及因過度捕撈造成牠們的食物短缺。這些都可能影響牠們的導航能力，使牠們迷失方向，或導致牠們變得太虛弱，而被沖刷至岸上。

受傷是另一個導致鯨魚擱淺的原因，與船隻和漁網的碰撞可能會造成無數的傷口，使牠們擱淺。除此之外，在水下的人為爆炸聲或地震的噪音都會嚴重損壞鯨魚的聽力，影響牠們導航、獵食與溝通的能力。

鯨魚也可能因為單純的導航失誤而擱淺，例如：游得太靠近海岸邊。有著浮木的淺灘、平緩的斜坡地形，都可能干擾鯨魚的回聲定位，使牠們缺

乏周遭的環境資訊。此外，不熟悉的海岸線與極端的天候狀況，皆是導致導航錯誤的潛在因素。

最後，牠們也可能因為社群之間的連結而擱淺。多種鯨魚都會與群體發展出緊密的社會連結，這有時候會導致鯨魚大量擱淺，因為當一隻鯨魚擱淺，群體的其他成員也會跟隨，這種現象最常發生在社會結構非常複雜的逆戟鯨身上。

1.	下列哪一張圖最能表達文中敘述的現象？	**評估詮釋**
	(A) 一群死鯨魚沈海底。	
	(B) 一群死鯨魚浮水面。	
	(C) 一群死鯨魚被網住。	
✓	(D) 一群死鯨魚擱淺沙灘。	

解析：
本文主要探討鯨魚擱淺的原因，本題在選出鯨魚被困住的場所，因此圖示應為一群鯨魚擱淺沙灘。故選 (D)。

2.	這篇文章主要在探討什麼？	**推論整合**
✓	(A) 鯨魚被沖上岸的原因。	
	(B) 鯨魚數量減少的原因。	
	(C) 漁夫獵捕鯨魚的方法。	
	(D) 鯨魚被困住的場所。	

解析：
(A) 本文主要討論鯨魚擱淺的原因，故選 (A)。
(B) 文中並未提到鯨魚數目是否減少。故 (B) 為非。
(C) 文中並未說明漁夫如何獵捕鯨魚。故 (C) 為非。
(D) 文中有提到鯨魚擱淺在沙灘這個場所，但並非主旨。故 (D) 為非。

3.	下列何者是鯨魚擱淺的最終原因？	**擷取訊息**
	(A) 牠們的健康狀況不佳。	
✓	(B) 牠們失去了導航能力。	
	(C) 牠們失去了聽力。	
	(D) 牠們離開了群體。	

解析：
由文中第二段的疾病、飢餓、重金屬，第三段聽力受損或第四段的淺灘、陌生環境，最後均因鯨魚失去導航能力導致擱淺，故選 (B)。

4.	下列何者可以從文章推斷出來？	**推論整合**
	(A) 許多鯨魚在海灘上自殺。	
	(B) 許多鯨魚是因為海底地震而死亡。	
	(C) 鯨魚會跟海豚與其他魚類一起遷徙。	
✓	(D) 海水被重金屬污染了。	

解析：
(A) 文中並未說明鯨魚擱淺是自殺。故 (A) 為非。
(B) 第三段指出海底地震傷害鯨魚聽力。此非直接促使鯨魚死亡的原因。故 (B) 為非。
(C) 第一段指出鯨魚成群遷徙，並非與海豚及魚類一起遷徙。故 (C) 為非。
(D) 第二段指出重金屬讓鯨魚生病，可知海洋受重金屬污染。故選 (D)。

Graphic Organizer

2. C　3. B　4. A　5. F　6. D

Reading Comprehension

1. B　2. D　3. C　4. A

小麥問題

麵包與義大利麵是許多人的主食，然而卻有研究指出，它們的原料——小麥——是造成許多健康問題的原因，困擾著現代社會。小麥屬於禾本科植物，人們栽種小麥是為了採收它的種子，以作為相對低廉的食物來源。儘管小麥的生產提供了世界人口負擔得起的能量來源，食用它也要付出一定的代價。

小麥中缺乏纖維的碳水化合物非常容易被人體吸收，因此會造成血糖急遽上升，而人體無法處理血液中過多的糖分，只好將其轉化為脂肪的形式儲存，進而導致肥胖。除此之外，這類的脂肪大部分都儲存在器官周圍，與心臟病的發生息息相關。

為了應對飆升的血糖，人體也必須分泌等量的胰島素，然而，過量的胰島素往往會導致細胞產生胰島素阻抗，因而造成第二型糖尿病。此外，血糖升高也會在皮膚中留下有毒的化學物質，導致膚質老化、乾燥並產生皺紋。

小麥也跟許多過敏症狀有關，會造成人體發炎，症狀包括起疹子、皮膚腫脹，甚至禿頭。

食用小麥也可能對心理造成影響，研究顯示，許多人從飲食中剔除小麥之後，不但心情變好、睡得更沉，而且專注力也提升了。然而，戒斷小麥的過程中也會面臨挑戰，大約有三成的人在飲食中去除小麥後，歷經了一些戒斷症狀，例如：極度疲倦、情緒不穩、頭腦昏沉等，這些症狀說明了小麥是會成癮的。而在某些案例中，小麥甚至會引起幻覺。一名長期受幻覺所苦的七十二歲婦人，在連續八天不吃小麥之後，幻覺的症狀不藥而癒。

不過，食用小麥也並非一無是處，研究指出，進食富含碳水化合物的食物，有立即提振心情的效果，但小麥並不是唯一含有碳水化合物的食物，總之，戒除小麥顯然是利大於弊。

1.	下列哪一圖表呈現正確的因果關係？	**擷取訊息**
	(A) wheat consumption 食用小麥 spikes in blood sugar 血糖驟升 extreme fatigue 極度疲倦 intolerances 過敏 inflammation 發炎	
✓	(B) spikes in blood sugar 血糖驟升 organ fat 器官脂肪 wrinkles 皺紋 type 2 diabetes 第二型糖尿病 insulin resistance 胰島素阻抗	
	(C) cutting carbohydrates 戒除碳水化合物 brain fog 頭腦昏沉 hallucinations 幻覺 toxic chemicals 有毒的化學物質 withdrawal symptoms 戒斷症狀	
	(D) wheat-free diets 無小麥飲食 better sleep 睡得更好 addiction 上癮 being overweight 體重過重 greater concentration 專注力提升	

解析：

(A) 由文章第五段，戒斷小麥的過程一開始才會有極度疲倦的症狀，而非食用小麥造成的情形。故 (A) 為非。
(B) 由文章第二段及第三段，血糖驟升會導致器官脂肪累積、第二型糖尿病、胰島素阻抗及皺紋。故選 (B)。
(C) 由文章第三段，在皮膚中留下有毒的化學物質是因食用碳水化合物造成血糖升高，而非戒除碳水化合物的情形。故 (C) 為非。
(D) 由文章第五段，無小麥飲食可讓心情變好、睡得更沉，而且專注力也提升了。而食用小麥才會上癮並導致肥胖。故 (D) 為非。

2.	這篇文章的目的為何？	**推論整合**
	(A) 說服讀者食用更便宜的食物。	
	(B) 教導讀者如何控制血糖。	
	(C) 告訴讀者心臟病的成因。	
✓	(D) 勸讀者不要食用小麥。	

解析：

由本文第一段最後一句 its consumption comes at a cost 和最後一段最後一句 it seems that the benefits of giving up wheat significantly outweigh the downsides 得知，作者認為食用小麥需付出不少代價，本文的目的是要勸讀者不要食用小麥。故選 (D)。

3.	下列何者並非用來支持作者論點的方法？ **評估詮釋**
	(A) 數據。
	(B) 研究。
✓	(C) 新聞報導。
	(D) 實例。

解析：
(A) 文中第五段有數據提到，約百分之三十的人戒吃小麥初期會出現脫癮癥狀。故 (A) 為非。
(B) 文中第一段及最後一段都有提到研究顯示。故 (B) 為非。
(C) 文中未提到新聞報導的部分。故選 (C)。
(D) 文中第四段列出發炎的例子。第五段有七十二歲婦人產生幻覺的例子。故 (D) 為非。

4.	根據此篇文章，下列敘述何者為真？ **擷取訊息**
✓	(A) 食用小麥的好處包括便宜的價格與對心情的正向影響。
	(B) 第二型糖尿病會使細胞對胰島素產生抗性。
	(C) 小麥中的碳水化合物會讓人們昏昏欲睡、不健康且衰老。
	(D) 人們要花很長的時間來適應沒有小麥的飲食習慣。

解析：
(A) 文中第一段指出小麥很便宜，最後一段指出吃碳水化合物心情會快速變好。故選 (A)。
(B) 由文章第三段，應為胰島素阻抗的細胞造成第二型糖尿病，因果相反。故 (B) 為非。
(C) 小麥中的碳水化合物會讓人不健康及老化，但文中未提到會讓人想睡，僅於第五段提到不吃小麥可提高睡眠品質。故 (C) 為非。
(D) 由文章第五段，飲食中戒除小麥需要時間，但並非很長的時間，文中的例子僅花八天。故 (D) 為非。

Graphic Organizer

2. contributes 3. similar 4. crucial 5. ensure
6. benefit 7. cruel 8. suffer 9. different
10. wastes 11. regulated 12. alternative

Reading Comprehension

1. A 2. D 3. C 4. B

動物實驗：贊成與反對

長久以來，動物實驗一直是頗具爭議的議題，一方面，它對醫療突破有所貢獻，能大大地造福人類；但另一方面，它卻要以動物受苦作為代價，因此，對於將產品試驗在動物身上，我們正面臨著道德上的兩難。無論你如何看動物實驗，總有某人或某事物需要犧牲，問題是——它是否值得。

基因上，人類約有百分之九十的 DNA 與老鼠相同，因此，老鼠的動物實驗提供了科學家一種在活體上實驗的方式，這些活體不僅具有健全的器官與系統，也擁有與人類相似的基因。此外，動物實驗也比其他方式更有效率，像老鼠等動物的壽命較短，使我們能在短時間內研究動物一生或甚至好幾世代上藥物和療法的功效。實際上，在多數救命藥物和療法的研發過程中，動物實驗一直扮演著至關重要的角色，上個世紀，幾乎所有的醫療突破皆是動物實驗的應用成果。

在臺灣，所有前景看好的新成分，從藥物到化妝品，都被規定必須經過動物實驗，以確保它們用在人體上是安全的。儘管動物實驗不可能找出所有有害物質，但它目前仍是降低人體危害的一個重要方法。再者，動物本身也能受惠於動物實驗，若沒有動物實驗，許多治療動物疾病的疫苗與療法也不會問世。

儘管利用動物做研究有許多優點，它確實也有一些缺點，其中最顯而易見的，是迫使生物進行這些實驗非常殘忍。動物和人類一樣，也會感到痛苦，所以為什麼讓牠們經歷這些是可以接受的呢？

動物實驗的另一個問題是可信度，就算有些動物與人類相似，但還是有所不同，動物可能不是理想的受試者。許多通過動物實驗的藥物，最終對人體並不安全，或者根本無效。這不僅浪費了動物的生命，也浪費了大量的金錢。除此之外，某些對人體既無害又有效的藥物，可能因為用在動物身上並不安全，而永遠不會被發現。

總而言之，動物實驗應該受到嚴格規範，研究人員必須盡可能以最人道的方式來對待受試動物，並審慎思考動物實驗的必要性。畢竟，某些重大醫療突破，原本可能不需動物實驗也能完成。希望能盡快找到替代方式，未來才能在相當程度上減少研究用途的動物數量。

1.	以下哪張圖與動物實驗無關？ **擷取訊息**
✓	(A) 貂皮大衣。
	(B) 吸菸的胸腔。
	(C) 化妝品 (乳液、口紅等)。
	(D) 藥片、藥丸、膠囊、針劑。

解析：
由文章第二段，動物實驗可用於研究活體器官，第三段指出在臺灣從藥品到化妝品均需經過動物實驗，因此 (A) 選項動物毛皮與動物實驗無關。故選 (A)。

2.	這篇文章未提及下列何者？ **評估詮釋**
	(A) 老鼠被用於實驗的原因。
	(B) 動物實驗的問題。
	(C) 動物實驗如何造福動物自己。
✓	(D) 科學家們如何操作動物實驗。

解析：
(A) 第二段提到老鼠約有百分之九十的基因與人類相同且壽命較短，因此常用來做動物實驗。
(B) 第四、五段指出動物實驗的問題，包括對動物相當殘忍，且可信度也不是絕對。
(C) 第三段說明動物實驗促成動物疫苗及療法的發明。
(D) 文中並未提到科學家如何做動物實驗。故選 (D)。

3.	下列何者最能描述作者對動物實驗的態度？ **推論整合**
	(A) 動物實驗太殘忍了，應該被禁止。
	(B) 動物實驗應被推廣到全世界。
✓	(C) 除非必要，否則應盡量避免動物實驗。
	(D) 做動物實驗只是為了人類和動物的利益。

解析：
由本文最後一段結論得知作者認為動物實驗應該嚴格規範，只有在必要的情況下，以人道的方式進行。故選 (C)。

4.	下列何者可從文章推斷？ **推論整合**
	(A) 若不使用動物實驗，科學家們就沒辦法達成醫療突破。
✓	(B) 反對動物實驗的人，非常關心動物的權益。
	(C) 越來越多國家都將立法禁止使用動物實驗。
	(D) 現在動物實驗是具爭議性的話題，但爭論將很快平息。

解析：
(A) 文中最後一段指出有些重要的醫學突破不需要動物實驗。故 (A) 為非。
(B) 反對者多要求以人道的方式進行動物實驗，因此推論他們重視動物的權益。故選 (B)。
(C) 文中並未提到越來越多國家將執行停止動物實驗的法律。故 (C) 為非。
(D) 第一段指出動物實驗長久以來一直是個有爭議的議題，迄今尚未有定論。故 (D) 為非。

Graphic Organizer

2. F　3. D　4. A　5. C　6. E

Reading Comprehension

1. B　2. C　3. C　4. D

禽流感與 SARS 的相似與相異

每年一到流感季節，媒體總會特別關注防疫議題。有時，不只是一般的感冒或流感在流傳，而是更嚴重的。提到超級病毒，很多在臺灣的人們腦中浮現的會是禽流感和 SARS (嚴重急性呼吸道症候群)。

禽流感與 SARS 的病毒有許多相似之處，兩者皆透過口鼻進入人體，並且會導致呼吸道的感染。它們引起的病徵也很類似，例如發燒和呼吸困難，而且，與一般感冒和多數其他類型的流感不同，這兩種病毒甚至可能致命。此外，這兩種病毒僅在動物之間傳播，在突變之後，才會傳染給人類。目前，尚沒有治癒禽流感或 SARS 的方法。

儘管禽流感與 SARS 有其相似之處，它們也有許多明顯的不同。如同禽流感字面上的意思，它是流感病毒的一種，而 SARS 的病毒，卻比較接近一般感冒。禽流感目前尚無法輕易由人類傳染給人類，但另一方面，SARS 可以在人類之間迅速傳開。不過，專家認為，若禽流感突變為可藉由人與人之間傳染，它的傳染性將大幅高過 SARS。儘管感染機率較低，禽流感卻比 SARS 致命得多。有高達五成的禽流感患者喪命，而 SARS 病人的死亡機率僅有一成。除此之外，最後一件確診的 SARS 病例發生在 2003 年，不像禽流感，近幾年有越來越多人感染的趨勢。

若你打算前往禽流感或 SARS 疫區旅遊，實行良好的衛生習慣是非常重要的。為了避免感染，你所能做最重要的事就是經常洗手、注意不要用手觸碰臉部，特別是眼睛跟鼻子。總之，對付這些致命病毒，再小心也不為過。

1.	以下哪張圖片為醫師對預防禽流感與 SARS 的建議？	**擷取訊息**
	(A) 禁止洗手。	
✓	(B) 禁止手揉眼睛。	
	(C) 禁止戴口罩。	
	(D) 禁止吃雞肉。	

解析：
由文章最後一段得知，預防禽流感和 SARS，應注意衛生、勤洗手、避免摸臉，尤其是鼻眼。故選 (B)。

2.	文中第二段到第三段關於禽流感與 SARS 的內容，其寫作結構為何？	**推論整合**
	(A) 利與弊。	
	(B) 因與果。	
✓	(C) 比較與對照。	
	(D) 分類。	

解析：
本文主要在比較禽流感與 SARS 的相同及相異之處。故選 (C)。

3.	文章中沒有提及以下哪一點？	**擷取訊息**
	(A) 人們感染禽流感死亡的百分比。	
	(B) 禽流感與 SARS 突變的後果。	
✓	(C) 一般感冒與 SARS 的異同之處。	
	(D) 避免感染禽流感及 SARS 採用的方法。	

解析：
(A) 文中第三段提到，高達五成的禽流感患者會死亡。故 (A) 為非。
(B) 文中第二段提到禽流感和 SARS 會突變成人傳人。故 (B) 為非。
(C) 本文比較禽流感與 SARS 的相同及相異之處，並未與一般感冒比較。故選 (C)。
(D) 文中最後一段有提到預防感染禽流感與 SARS 的方法。故 (D) 為非。

4.	從文章中可推斷出下列何者？ **推論整合**
	(A) 現在全球都能找到禽流感及 SARS 的病毒。
	(B) 患有禽流感及 SARS 的人必死無疑。
	(C) 禽流感較為致命，因為它比 SARS 更常突變。
✓	(D) 禽流感及 SARS 的病毒皆會攻擊病患的呼吸道系統。

解析：

(A) 由文章第三段最後一句，最後一個 SARS 病例出現在 2003 年，因此現今並非全球都有。故 (A) 為非。
(B) 由文章第三段，得到禽流感或 SARS 並非一定會死亡。故 (B) 為非。
(C) 由文章第三段，禽流感致命率更高，因為人傳人傳染力高，並非因為比 SARS 更常突變。故 (C) 為非。
(D) 由文章第二段，禽流感和 SARS 病毒會造成呼吸系統的感染。故選 (D)。

Graphic Organizer

2. B 3. D 4. E 5. H 6. A 7. F 8. C

Reading Comprehension

1. B 2. A 3. C 4. A

會吃塑膠的蟲？

關於垃圾處理，隨著食用塑膠的毛毛蟲被發現，將可能出現嶄新的突破。最初由一位科學家——一位業餘的養蜂者——無意間發現蠟蛾幼蟲吃穿了他的一些塑膠袋。這種毛毛蟲能蛀蝕聚乙烯，聚乙烯正是人們最常用的塑膠種類之一。自這項發現開始，有人便推測，或許可以利用毛毛蟲來處理我們每年傾倒在垃圾掩埋場裡的塑膠，不幸的是，若為此目的繁殖蠟蛾，將會遇上一些困難。

每隻幼蟲一日約可吃掉 2 毫克的塑膠，以此來看，光是 1 公噸的塑膠分量，我們就需要超過 100 萬隻毛蟲，才能在一年內咀嚼完。考量到光是英國每年就倒掉超過 200 萬公噸的塑膠，需要好幾兆的蠟蛾幼蟲，才能對塑膠垃圾量造成明顯的改變，這顯然不切實際。

此提議的第二個問題則是蠟蛾本身，正如其名，蠟蛾的幼蟲以蜂窩內的蠟質蜂巢為食，蠟蛾會在蜂窩內產下 300 至 600 顆卵，孵化的幼蟲可能會從內部將蜂窩完全破壞，如果這些為數眾多的敵害被允許蔓延，許許多多生活在蜂窩內的蜜蜂，將受到威脅。由於蜜蜂在人類食物的收成產量中扮演著不可或缺的角色，而牠們的數量又已面臨危機，繁殖好幾兆的蠟蛾大概不是最好的主意。

不過，這項新發現也並非毫無貢獻。最近，一群日本科學家發現了一種細菌，可以吃掉用來製造汽水瓶和礦泉水瓶的塑膠。事實上，早在 2014 年，人們就發現另一種蠟蛾——印度穀蛾的消化系統中，也有能夠分解聚乙烯的細菌。這表示蠟蛾之所以能夠分解聚乙烯，主要與牠們身上的這種細菌有關，而非蠟蛾本身。科學家相信，透過了解這種細菌分解聚乙烯的方式，將能找到替代方案，來解決塑膠汙染的問題。或許在不久的將來，塑膠汙染不再會威脅我們的地球。

1.	下圖為蠟蛾的生命週期，哪個階段有助於我們擺脫塑膠垃圾？	**擷取訊息**
	(A) 卵。	
✓	(B) 毛毛蟲。	
	(C) 蛹。	
	(D) 蛾。	

解析：

由文章第一段，會吃塑膠的為蠟蛾的幼蟲階段，即是毛毛蟲時期。故選 (B)。

2.	文章第二段最後一句中的「This」，代指的是什麼？	**評估詮釋**
✓	(A) 飼養蛾的幼蟲以咀嚼塑膠。	
	(B) 傾倒 200 萬公噸的塑膠。	
	(C) 使蜜蜂群處於險境。	
	(D) 處理塑膠垃圾。	

解析：

文中前面指出，需要 100 萬隻蠟蛾的幼蟲一年才能吃掉 1 公噸的塑膠，而光英國一年就製造了 200 萬公噸的塑膠垃圾，因此至少需要數兆隻蠟蛾幼蟲才夠解決塑膠問題。因此養蠟蛾幼蟲來處理塑膠垃圾是非常不實際的。故選 (A)。

3.	根據文章，下列敘述何者為真？	**擷取訊息**
	(A) 蛾的幼蟲以蜜蜂為食。	
	(B) 蛾的毛毛蟲長大會變成幼蟲。	
✓	(C) 聚乙烯是一種常見的塑膠。	
	(D) 印度穀蛾並不是蠟蛾。	

解析：

(A) 蛾的幼蟲以蜂巢上的蜂蠟為主食，並非蜜蜂。故 (A) 為非。
(B) 毛毛蟲就是蛾的幼蟲。故 (B) 為非。
(C) 由文中第一段，聚乙烯是一種常見的塑膠。故選 (C)。
(D) 由文中第四段，印度穀蛾也是一種蠟蛾。故 (D) 為非。

4.	我們能從文章中推論出什麼？	**推論整合**
✓	(A) 數量龐大的蠟蛾帶來的傷害將大過於好處。	
	(B) 研究蛾的行為可以解決塑膠汙染的議題。	
	(C) 比起其他蠟蛾，印度穀蛾可以吃掉較多的聚乙烯。	
	(D) 作者對此發現持負面態度。	

解析：

(A) 由文章第三段，數量龐大的蠟蛾會對蜜蜂造成威脅，而蜜蜂對人類食物供應更重要，因此大量蠟蛾造成的傷害大於益處。故選 (A)。
(B) 文中並未提到蠟蛾的行為。故 (B) 為非。
(C) 由文章第四段，印度穀蛾是利用消化系統中的細菌分解聚乙烯，但文中並未提到印度穀蛾分解塑膠垃圾的數量。故 (C) 為非。
(D) 作者對這項發現並非抱持悲觀態度，最後一段指出它並非沒有前景。透過了解細菌分解聚乙烯的方式，可能會找到替代方案，來解決塑膠汙染的問題。故 (D) 為非。

Graphic Organizer

2. A　3. B　4. F　5. D　6. E

Reading Comprehension

1. B　2. A　3. C　4. D

動物學校

很久以前，世界上動物們開會並下定決心要處理困擾著現代世界的所有問題。他們建造了一所新學校，無論學生是哪種動物，這所學校都會一視同仁地教導他們跑步、爬樹、飛翔和游泳。

鴨同學本來是名傑出的泳者，實力甚至勝過他的老師，但他的飛行成績僅勉強及格，跑步則是糟糕透頂。由於他跑得實在太差了，下課後必須留下來練習，為了跟上其他同學，他甚至必須放棄游泳課。一段時間之後，他長蹼的雙腳因為練習飽受摧殘，最後，他只是一名普普通通的泳者，不過因為他的跑步成績及格了，所以除了他自己，其他人也不大在乎了。

開學的時候，兔子同學是全班跑得最快的，但經過好多好多個小時的游泳補救教學，她精神崩潰了，必須請假離開學校一陣子。松鼠同學原本是位很有天分的爬樹高手，但卻因為飛行課程而變得極度沮喪。他被迫從地面往上飛，而不是從樹頂往下飛，因此，他的肌肉因為過度運動而嚴重抽筋。最後，他在爬樹課拿了 C，跑步課拿了 D。

老鷹同學不大理會學校的規則，在爬樹課上，她打敗了其他動物到達樹頂，但沒有照著該用的方法，於是被嚴厲地懲罰了。到了學年尾聲，一隻不尋常的鰻魚因為游泳游得好，而且會跑步、爬樹，飛行也會一點，得到了全校最高的平均分數，並以最高榮譽畢業。

然而，也有動物從來不去學校，草原犬鼠抗議學程中沒有挖洞跟挖隧道的課程，他們和美洲旱獺還有囊地鼠一起創辦了一間很成功的私立學校，專門收擅長挖掘的學生。

這則寓言故事強調了擁抱個體專長的重要性，並警世，學校不該強迫任何人去達成那些主觀設立的標準，而犧牲了各自的天分。就像老鷹就該飛翔一樣，歌者當歌，作家應該寫作，而善於建造的人就該建造。

1.	根據文章的描述，這份成績單最有可能屬於哪隻動物的？ 爬樹：C 跑步：C 飛翔：C 游泳：B	**推論整合**
	(A) 鰻魚。	
✓	(B) 鴨子。	
	(C) 兔子。	
	(D) 松鼠。	

解析：

(A) 由文章第四段，鰻魚游泳游得好，應該得 A，而且其他也不錯，推斷不可能是鰻魚。故 (A) 為非。
(B) 由文章第二段，鴨子勉強通過了跑步，游泳能力變成普通，因此推斷非常可能是鴨子。故選 (B)。
(C) 由文章第三段，兔子游泳一直補考，最後精神崩潰，所以游泳不可能得 B，推斷不是兔子的成績單。故 (C) 為非。
(D) 由文章第三段，松鼠爬樹得到 C，跑步得到 D，因此不可能是松鼠。故 (D) 為非。

2.	到了學期末，動物們怎麼了？	**推論整合**
✓	(A) 他們什麼也不擅長。	
	(B) 他們的考試成績全都及格了。	
	(C) 他們全都受了重傷。	
	(D) 他們輟學了。	

解析：

(A) 學期結束時，這些動物因為學習其不擅長的科目，而荒廢原本擅長的科目。故選 (A)。
(B) 文中並未提及所有學生的考試都及格。故 (B) 為非。
(C) 並非所有動物都嚴重受傷。故 (C) 為非。
(D) 並非所有動物都輟學。故 (D) 為非。

3.	以下關於第一所學校的描述，何者為非？	擷取訊息
	(A) 學校強迫所有學生都要修所有課程。	
	(B) 學校不在乎每位學生的差異。	
✓	(C) 藉由老師的幫助，學生們發展了他們潛在的能力。	
	(D) 如果學生沒有遵守規定就會受到處罰。	

解析：

(A) 文章第一段提到學校會一視同仁地教導他們跑步、爬樹、飛翔和游泳。因此要求學生修習所有必修課程。故 (A) 為對。
(B) 由文章第二及第三段，學校不在乎學生個別差異。故 (B) 為對。
(C) 文中未提到學生在老師幫助下發展他們的潛能，因此錯誤。故選 (C)。
(D) 由文章第四段，學生不遵守規定會被處罰，例如老鷹。故 (D) 為對。

4.	為什麼土撥鼠成立的新學校是所成功的學校？	評估詮釋
	(A) 因為它是一間昂貴的私立學校。	
	(B) 因為它只教導有才能的學生。	
	(C) 因為只有具備天賦的學生才能念這所學校。	
✓	(D) 因為學生在那裡得以發展他們的天分。	

解析：

土撥鼠學校是為有挖掘專長的動物而設，因此學生只要繼續發展自己的專長就好。故選 (D)。

Unit 12

Graphic Organizer

2. withered 3. elixir 4. fight 5. old 6. lesson

Reading Comprehension

1. B 2. B 3. D 4. C

Heidegger 醫生的實驗

Heidegger 醫生是一位古怪的獨居老人，總是待在神秘的實驗室裡，把時間花在做實驗和他的眾多研究上。有一天，他邀請了四位老朋友來參與一個開創性的實驗。

這些訪客包含三位男士與一位女士，都曾因不檢點的生活遭人非議，並在晚年時為他們的罪過付出代價。除此之外，這三位男士都曾是那位女士的情人，並為了得到她的愛互相爭鬥。

Heidegger 醫生帶這四位訪客來到他的實驗室，要他們圍坐在房間中央的桌子，桌子的中間擺了一只精緻的花瓶，裡面裝著閃閃發亮的液體。接著，Heidegger 醫生向他們展示了一朵乾燥且枯萎的玫瑰，並把它放進花瓶中。就在它的莖碰到那液體後不久，那朵玫瑰開始產生變化，過沒多久變得彷彿換了一朵剛剪下來的玫瑰一樣。

四名訪客都吃了一驚但也對其中的真實性存疑，覺得是一場騙局。Heidegger 醫生宣稱瓶中的水來自青春之泉，並遞給每人一杯，他告訴他的訪客這杯水將恢復他們的青春，但他們要記住，不要重蹈覆轍年輕時的錯誤，他們也都同意了。

他們抱著疑慮喝下了水，沒有多久他們的外表便開始轉變，各個看起來年輕了三十歲。一股興奮感湧上，他們喝下了更多，現在，他們已回到青春歲月的巔峰。活力充沛的他們開始思考接下來該做些什麼，然而，他們的所做所為和之前並無二致，尤有甚者，男士們對於那位重獲青春的美麗女子更有興致了，開始為了她的垂青而互相競爭，情況演變成一場惡鬥，在衝突中，花瓶被打碎了，長生不老藥也灑了出來。

剎那間，那朵玫瑰開始枯萎，而訪客們也一樣。藥水的效力是如此短暫，使四個人感到前所未有的絕望。那天，對於人性 Heidegger 醫生學到了一課，大多數人即使有機會重回年輕時代，仍然會犯下相同的錯誤；這四名訪客什麼也沒學到，反而下定決心要啟程尋找青春之泉。

1.	下列哪一張圖最能表現第三段的場景？	**擷取訊息**
	(A) Heidegger 醫生站著，手中拿著一個精緻的花瓶，花瓶裡插著一朵枯萎的玫瑰，三個老男人，一個老女人，圍著房間中央的桌子坐。	
✓	(B) Heidegger 醫生站著，手中拿著一朵枯萎的玫瑰，三個老男人，一個老女人，圍著房間中央的桌子坐，桌子中央有一個精緻的花瓶。	
	(C) Heidegger 醫生坐在房間中央的桌前，手中拿著一朵枯萎的玫瑰，三個老男人，一個老女人，圍著 Heidegger 醫生站著，桌子上有一個精緻的花瓶。	
	(D) Heidegger 醫生站著，手中拿著一朵枯萎的玫瑰，三個老男人，一個老女人，圍著 Heidegger 醫生站著，房間右側靠牆有一張桌子，桌子上有一個精緻的花瓶。	

解析：
由第三段得知 Heidegger 醫生手中拿著一朵枯萎的玫瑰花，三位年長的男士和一位年長的女士圍著房間中間的桌子而坐，桌子中央有一個精緻的花瓶。故選 (B)。

2.	四名訪客一開始對 Heidegger 醫生的實驗有什麼反應？	**擷取訊息**
	(A) 他們很期待。	
✓	(B) 他們不抱期待。	
	(C) 他們迫不及待地想嘗試。	
	(D) 他們毫不遲疑地就喝了。	

解析：
由第四段得知他們的第一反應是震驚、懷疑並認為那是騙局，(A)(C)(D) 均表迫切地想嘗試，(B) 他們表示不抱期待。故選 (B)。

3.	下面哪一敘述最符合本文的主題？	**推論整合**
	(A) 好心有好報。	
	(B) 蘿蔔青菜，各有所好。	
	(C) 要怎麼收穫，先那麼栽。	
✓	(D) 江山易改，本性難移。	

解析：
本文主旨為「人就算有機會回到過去，也仍會重蹈覆轍」，江山易改，本性難移。故選 (D)。

4.	這個故事並沒有談到實驗的哪一個部分？	**評估詮釋**
	(A) 過程。	
	(B) 結果。	
✓	(C) 目的。	
	(D) 受試者。	

解析：
本文第三、四、五段均為實驗過程，最後一段有實驗結果，而四位老人為實驗對象，但文中並未提及做此實驗的目的。故選 (C)。

Graphic Organizers for Effective Reading!

- 精選 18 種實用圖形組織圖，
  最常用的 G.O. 通通有！
- 全書共 12 課，多元文體搭配 12 種圖形組織圖，
  閱讀素材通通有！
- 每課搭配 G.O. 練習題與 4 題閱讀測驗，
  組織架構、閱讀練習通通有！
- 閱讀測驗題標記測驗重點，
  隨時檢視閱讀成效！
- 貼心整理文章生難字及片語，
  文本與單字左右對照，字彙能力通通有！

「英文閱讀G.O., G.O., G.O.!」
與「翻譯與解析」不分售
211-80291G